MW01286602

WHO
SHOT
THE
SPEAKER?

Christopher B. Emery

BookLocker
Trenton, Georgia

Print ISBN: 978-1-958890-62-2
Ebook ISBN: 979-8-88531-564-7

Christopher B. Emery
Manns Choice, PA
WhiteHouseUsher@gmail.com
www.WhiteHouseUsher.com

Ordering Information:
Quantity sales: Special discounts are available on quantity purchases by corporations, associations, and others. For details, contact the publisher at the address above.
Orders by US trade bookstores and wholesalers. Please visit: www.WhiteHouseUsher.com.

Printed on acid-free paper.

Publisher's Cataloging-in-Publication data
Emery, Christopher B.
Who Shot the Speaker? / Christopher B Emery
p. cm.
1. The main category of the book—Fiction F0000.A0 A00 2010
299.000 00–dc22 2010999999
Library of Congress Control Number: 2021915141

First Edition

Dedicated to:

Katie
Waverly
Parker

and

Isabelle

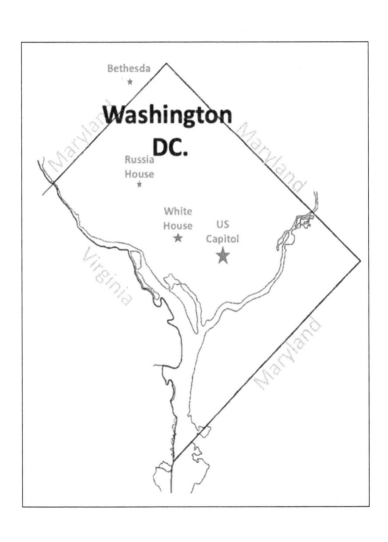

Prologue

Who Shot the Speaker? is the second in the debut series and follows *Who Killed the President?*, a Washington, DC whodunit authored by a true White House insider, former White House Usher Chris Emery. The novel revolves around the shocking murder of the president of the United States, which occurred right inside the White House. Almost as shocking, details emerge implicating a member of the White House Ushers Office. The evidence seems overwhelming, and the case is considered open and closed. If only the rest of the world knew the intrigue and subterfuge…everything that went on behind the scenes and just beneath the glossy white veneer of America's most venerated house. In *Who Killed the President?*, Chief Usher Bartholomew Winston, a fifty-year veteran of the White House, works with investigators to uncover the truth, even if it means diving headfirst into dangerous political waters to uncover it.

The sequel, *Who Shot the Speaker?*, can be enjoyed independently. For those who are new to the series or in need of a brief refresher, I've offered a brief summary of the main characters below:

Jonathan Cartwright: a veteran with the Department of Justice and lead investigator into the assassination of President John Blake in *Who Killed the President?*.

Elizabeth Gentry: initially the vice president, but as a result of President John Blake's assassination, in *Who Killed the President?* Gentry became the youngest and first female president in US history. A captivating and dynamic orator, super-intelligent, and stunningly beautiful, she is wildly popular among the American public. But she has a dark side.

Annika Antonov: Russian FSB agent (the successor agency to the old KGB). A hardened senior agent, she's a calculating, cold-blooded killer who also has charm and a heart.

Bartholomew Winston: the main character in *Who Killed the President?* A White House Usher for over fifty years, Winston formed the small but effective investigative group that helped solve the case.

Frank Osborne: a successful man whose career in Washington has encompassed a variety of roles, from a Secret Service agent to a US attorney and finally a K Street lawyer. Renowned for representing corporate and political leaders in various noteworthy cases, Frank has been instrumental in providing behind-the-scenes political strategies to high office holders on both sides of the aisle. In ***Who Killed the President?*** Frank worked closely with Bartholomew Winston and Jonathan Cartwright.

Chapter 1

Saturday, October 29
Omni Springs Resort, Bedford, Pennsylvania

The sun had burned off the last of the morning mist. The surrounding Allegheny Mountains, their fall foliage at their peak, provided a breathtaking view.

Gus had been in position since before sunrise. His shoulders and knees ached, and his neck was stiff from lying motionless on his stomach for nearly three hours.

He sighed. Back in Vietnam, this kind of twelve-to-fifteen-hour-long routine had never brought any discomfort. Now, just a few hours were torture. "God, I'm getting too old for this," he muttered, struggling to focus on the beauty and tranquility of the golf course below instead of his aching bones. It didn't help—he still hurt all over.

Gus was still lost in thought when he heard a voice in his earpiece. He reacted on instinct, pressing his hand over his ear in time to hear the message repeated:

"Repeat. We're good to go. Principal is wearing white visor, pink top, and white pants." Gus caught a heavy foreign accent and raised an eyebrow. He reached down to his waist and pressed the transmit button on his walkie-talkie twice to confirm receipt of the message.

Wearing his camo Woodland Ghillie Suit, which blended him superbly with his surroundings, he was practically invisible. He shifted his head in one deft motion, peering through the Nightforce BEAST 5-25x56mm scope of his Accuracy International AT .308 rifle, then fine-tuning the focus until he had a clear, unobstructed view of the fourth tee. He gazed on through his scope, observing four golf carts pull up. Several individuals disembarked from the vehicles, with three approaching the tee. His target, the Speaker of the House, was easy to spot given her bright pink windbreaker. The speaker's two-person security detail positioned themselves twenty feet apart from one another, a full twenty feet behind the tee.

Gus' eyes fell on the gallery of three dozen spectators, and he tensed. He had not calculated this as a factor. After taking a deep breath to settle his nerves, he checked his range finder, confirming the target was

457 yards from his position. There was the typical six-mile-an-hour breeze coming out of the west, which he felt gently blowing onto his face. The sun was at his back, bright and shining; he had been extra careful in his preparations to ensure nothing in his immediate surroundings would cause any reflection that could give away his position. He double-checked his ballistics chart, making the final adjustments for distance and windage, and then waited until he was sure none of the spectators were in the way of his shot.

Gus slowly squeezed the trigger, the report of the 150-grain .308 bullet initially muffled by the AI tactical sound suppressor, but then, the crack of the bullet breaking the sound barrier echoed loudly through the valley. Gus peered through his rifle scope, expecting to see the burst of gore as the speaker's head exploded, but instead was stunned as the screen of the golf cart behind the speaker shattered. He had missed! The scene instantly became mass bedlam. The speaker's protective detail immediately reacted based on their training. They jumped on top of her, knocking her to the ground and covering her. Spectators panicked, many screaming and running in all directions. Gus grimaced; there was no opportunity for a second shot. He hastily grabbed his equipment and scrambled to get out from beneath the brush. As he started to stand, something hard slammed into the side of his head; he fell to the ground unconscious.

Lucifer and Elsa, a local couple in their mid-forties who had fallen on hard times, were sneaking around the golf course, gathering balls that they could sell. For a while, they had been making good use of a TaylorMade 3-iron club they had swiped one night after hours to dig up hidden balls. They heard the shot, then saw the rifle; a quick-thinking Lucifer dropped his bottle of Jack Daniel's and crept up behind the distracted sniper, using the golf club to clobber Gus over the head. He then yelled at Elsa to take a pic and call the news, drunkenly slurring, "Here goes me bashing the motherfucker!" He struck a triumphant pose as he stood over Gus, about to strike again, but then held off as he looked down at the fallen man. "Sonbitch, I ain't kilt ya yet!"

Lucifer was a giant of a man; his long, straggly hair and full beard made him resemble a hairy ape. Sinking to one knee, he examined Gus for signs of life and found a pulse just as Gus was starting to stir. Lucifer looked at Elsa. "Quick, babe, call Channel 8. Tell 'em you just witnessed a local hero stop this bastard from killing someone!" Lucifer then put Gus in a headlock and dragged the sniper onto the nearby golf course while waving his free arm over his head. Elsa followed along while continuing to search her phone for the local TV affiliate.

Chapter 2
Two days earlier

Thursday, October 27
US Capitol Building, Washington, DC

It was early afternoon, and House Speaker Suzanne Montgomery sat on the sofa in her large office adjacent to the House Chamber in the US Capitol. With a pile of envelopes on her lap, she slipped off her heels and propped her feet up on the coffee table in front of her. An attractive and fit woman in her late fifties, Speaker Montgomery had medium-length brown hair that was starting to show more and more gray. As always, she was exceptionally well-dressed, but the job was taking its toll; she often looked tired.

Her cell phone rang. She smiled as she recognized the number and answered: "How's my favorite senator? I sure hope your day is better than mine."

"You're not going to believe this... I'm so mad, I can't even see straight. Your and my nemesis, that conniving, plotting, evil Elizabeth Gentry, our president for the past eight months, and hopefully not for the next eight! She had the audacity to call me, and in this sickeningly sweet voice, told me that if I would get on board with her, she would nominate me to fill her vacancy for vice president. I was stunned. She went on about what a great team we would make. Before I could even think of anything to say to that, she added that if I didn't accept her nomination, she would veto my jobs bill. I lost it…asked if she was insane. She then became ice-cold and told me her veto would be made official tonight and wished me luck surviving my term. Oh, my God! The woman is certifiable! I spent fourteen months on that bill. Former President Blake, God rest his soul, had promised me he would pass it. Heck, he helped me write it! I'm fed up with her. Plus, I'm getting all sorts of intel about the kind of stuff she's up to—it's all beyond outrageous. If I can get proof, I'm going to launch an investigation." The senator exhaled loudly. "Sorry, I didn't mean to go on for so long. Tell me, how is your day?"

Speaker Montgomery closed her eyes and slowly shook her head. "Oh, my God, Ron. I too am in shock. I'm so sorry. If it's any consolation, she's been all over me too, coming at me in all directions, always with the intent of making me look bad. I'm not sure what I'm going to do. Did you see her latest polling numbers?"

"Yes, unbelievable," the senator agreed. "She's now outpolling former President Blake, and most experts agree that he was the best president we have had in over one hundred years!"

"I need a drink!" exclaimed Suzanne. "Maybe we can get together later. I've got to handle some things."

"Yes, let's do that. Talk to you later."

The speaker ended the call, tossed her phone on the couch next to her, and then paused for a moment, scanning the pile of mail on her lap. She purposely dropped the largest envelope on top of the end table closest to her, then stared at the next piece of mail for a moment. *Strange*, she thought, *it's not addressed, just blank*. She opened and shook the envelope, and a small rectangular piece of black plastic fell into her lap. The speaker looked at the strange object for a moment, then reached for her cell phone and called her chief of staff. "Jennifer, are you free? I've got something we need to look at."

Moments later, Chief of Staff Jennifer Largent gave a courtesy knock and, without awaiting a response, opened the door and walked in. Largent, a tall, thin woman in her mid-forties with medium-length dark hair, wore the same darkness under her eyes as many of Suzanne's staff, a side effect of the strain of working long hours for the Speaker of the House. Jennifer Largent had served as Suzanne Montgomery's chief of staff for the past twelve years. Largent donned a serious look and asked, "What have we got?"

Speaker Montgomery, holding up the item between her thumb and forefinger, replied, "I have no idea. What am I supposed to do with this? It arrived in an internal envelope with no address."

Jennifer's eyes scanned the device. "Oh, it's a microSD card. Your computer has a reader. Let's go see what's on it."

Intrigued by this ominous device, Montgomery slowly rose, leaving her shoes behind and heading over to her desk, sinking into the seat behind it. Jennifer dragged a chair next to hers, then plugged the microSD into the reader. The automatic security scan took less than ten seconds; after that, they found a single file titled: Blake Assassination Investigation.

The speaker's eyes went wide. "Holy cow! Let's open it!"

Jennifer double-clicked on the PDF file, and they both stared in silence as the title page appeared.

-TOP SECRET-
EYES ONLY: US ATTORNEY GENERAL

REPORT ON THE ASSASSINATION OF
PRESIDENT JOHN BLAKE

DRAFT
INTERNAL REVIEW

Prepared by
Jonathan Cartwright
LEAD INVESTIGATOR

DEPARTMENT OF JUSTICE:
NATIONAL SECURITY DIVISION

For the next ninety minutes, the two scanned the 180-page, double-spaced report.

"Wow!" breathed Montgomery. "This is remarkable. We've been waiting for months… The damn DOJ has been so slow." She thought for a moment, then said, "Here's what I want us to do: Rewrite this report to make it seem as if it originated from my office. What's on my calendar?"

"You have a Greek reception in the Rayburn House Office Building that started at 3 p.m.," Jennifer recited from memory.

Montgomery made a face. "Forget that. What about tomorrow?"

"Tomorrow is Friday," Jennifer recalled, "and you and the president are giving an address at the Naval Academy in Annapolis."

"Ugh! I hate attending events with her, but I really need to be there. What do I have the next few days?"

Jennifer lifted the iPad in her hands, checking her calendar app. "Saturday, you're doing a celebrity golf tournament in your home state of Pennsylvania. Your tee time is 10 a.m. Tom Selleck and Kevin Costner are in your group."

Speaker Montgomery smiled. "Mmm, nice… A ménage à trois!"

Jennifer barked out a half-laugh. "Stop!" She then continued, "Okay, Monday, you are in committee all day. Tuesday morning, you are chairing the Ways and Means investigation hearing, and as of right now, Tuesday afternoon from two on, you are free."

Montgomery nodded. "Perfect! Schedule a press conference for Tuesday at 4 p.m. Leak to the press that I am releasing my internal investigation into the Blake assassination. This is just what this office needs. We've been screwed by the House Minority, the Senate, and most of all, that bitch president. It's time we got some positive attention and expose the president for who she really is!"

"Okay," Jennifer agreed enthusiastically. "I'm on it!"

"Oh, and send me the latest draft of tomorrow's address. And Jennifer, it's the Naval Academy. I need to come across as a hawk!"

Chapter 3

Thursday, October 27
The White House

It was just after 5 o'clock, and President Elizabeth Gentry sat in the West Sitting Hall of the White House private residence. The late day sun shone brightly through the large, majestic half-circle window behind the sofa, where she currently sat, still clad in the black slacks and black turtleneck sweater she had worn to the Oval Office. Her matching black jacket was draped over a nearby chair, and she had just kicked off her Sarah Flint pumps, which lay on the floor near her. Having removed her contacts, she was now wearing glasses, and with the late afternoon light, her intense gray eyes now appeared a soft gray green in color. At 5'8' and 130 pounds she had a naturally athletic body. Her face was thin, and she had a small nose and full lips. Her dark hair was tied back in a simple style, and though she was tired, she looked young, vibrant, and beautiful.

President Gentry's burner cell phone buzzed; she pulled the phone out of her small purse, seeing a text from Roman Mirov. She frowned, mulling over everything she knew about the high-level Russian oligarch who, years ago, had amassed a fortune as a commodities and shipping magnate. Over the past twenty years, he'd also become a close confidant of Vladimir Putin and was currently Putin's designee to run the Washington, DC operations of the Federal Security Service (FSB, Federal'naya Sluzhba Bezopasnosti), the successor to the old KGB. Mirov, a jovial, rotund man in his approximate mid-fifties, enjoyed good times and good vodka. An ongoing classified investigation had recently revealed that Mirov had been responsible for huge contributions to Elizabeth Gentry's three congressional campaigns and, more recently, to the Blake-Gentry campaign for president.

The president read the text: *I'm near the northwest Gate, I need to meet with you—urgent.*

The president responded to the text: *I'll have you cleared for 6 p.m.*

The president then called her chief of staff. "Wendy, I need Roman Mirov cleared for the northwest gate. I will meet with him in the Executive Residence. This meeting is OTR [off the record]."

Wendy replied over the phone, "I'm taking care of it now."

Ten minutes later, the phone on the end table rang. As soon as the president answered, the administration operator said, "I have the Ushers Office on the line."

"Yes," the president affirmed, waiting.

"Mrs. President, this is James Allen in the Ushers Office. I have Mr. Roman Mirov here to see you."

"Bring him up. Oh, and James, I don't want anyone on the second floor. Please tell the butlers and the chef to hold my dinner until 7:30." The president hung up before James could respond.

Thirty seconds later, the president stood. After hearing the elevator doors open, she walked and met Usher James Allen, who led Roman Mirov into the West Sitting Hall.

The president nodded at the White House's newest guest. "Roman, good to see you. Come, have a seat." She led him into the West Sitting Hall, where she resettled onto the couch in the exact same position as before, then motioned for Roman to take a seat close to her. "What's urgent?"

Mirov sat on the last couch cushion on the right. "Mrs. President, I have some bad news."

Gentry motioned with her hand. "Go on."

Mirov's expression was dour. "As you know, we were successful in obtaining the assassination report, which I believe you have now read."

The president's mouth was a thin line. "Yes, of course, I read it. Go on. What's your news?"

Mirov continued, "As you directed, I made arrangements to get the report to the chairman of the Judiciary Committee."

"Yes, I talked to the chairman an hour ago," replied President Gentry. "He informed me he never received it."

"Correct, Madam President. It was somehow redirected to the speaker's office."

The president glared at Mirov. "What did you just say?!"

Mirov shifted in his seat. "I cannot explain it, Madam President. Somehow the report got sent to the office of the speaker."

The president jolted to her feet and yelled, "Are you fucking serious?!"

Mirov glanced down. "Madam President, I'm sincerely sorry. I don't know how this happened."

In a rage, the president began pacing back and forth, shouting intermittently at the man on the couch. "*Jesus...* If you're right, then this is a colossal failure on your part! Do you realize the impact of the speaker having this report? Are you prepared to spend the rest of your fucking life at Guantanamo?!"

Mirov quietly absorbed her rant. Seeming to have finally spent the bulk of her rage, the president leaned on the back of a nearby chair, shaking her head, and took a deep breath. "Has there been any reaction from the speaker?"

Mirov licked his bottom lip before answering, "We know she scheduled a press conference for Tuesday afternoon, and she leaked to the press that she would be presenting 'her' findings on the assassination."

The president's eyes rolled up in her head. "Oh, my God. I am so angry, I cannot see straight. Damn it to hell, you leave me with no other choice: You need to eliminate the speaker, and I also need Jonathan Cartwright eliminated. Am I clear?"

Mirov nodded. "Understood. I'll take care of it."

Gentry heaved out a long breath. "Okay, Roman, get the hell out of here. Keep me informed of your progress."

Chapter 4

Friday, October 28
Undisclosed location, Washington, DC

Victor Orloff, a high-level Russian FSB agent, had been working undercover in Washington for the past eight months. He had just received high-priority instructions from his boss, Roman Mirov. The order was clear: urgent, top priority, eliminate the Speaker of the House. Victor was able to quickly confirm that the very next day, the Speaker of the House, Suzanne Montgomery, would be participating in a charity golf tournament hosted by the Omni Resort Hotel in Bedford, Pennsylvania. The Omni was 144 miles away in West Central Pennsylvania. Due to the short notice and immediate need, Victor Orloff decided to rely on a local asset to handle the kill.

...

West Central Pennsylvania

The "local asset," Gus Jones, a sixty-eight-year-old former marine sniper, had served in Vietnam at the very end of the war, and over the past several years, had done a few jobs for the Russian FSB. He'd proven reliable. That, and the fact that he conveniently resided in the tiny town of New Baltimore, Pennsylvania, where he rented a run-down trailer, helped secure the job for him. Gus was a loner but known locally for having set the record for the longest whitetail deer kill at 823 yards.

At noon, Gus rode his Harley exactly twenty-one miles east, stopping in the vicinity of the opulent Bedford Omni resort. To anyone watching him, he was an old man, perhaps seeming a bit spry for his years, taking a brisk stroll. His "stroll" lasted two hours—time well spent surveying the area around the golf course, scoping out the optimal sniper location. Confident with his choice of location, he marked his spot using the what3words app, identifying the locale as "traded.spills.faxing". He then forwarded it to his contact and confirmed he would handle the job the next morning for the agreed price of $50,000.

Chapter 5

Present Time
Sunday, November 1
Cape Idokopas, Russia

Fifteen hundred miles due south of Moscow sat the Black Sea resort town of Gelendzhik. A forty-minute drive down the coast from Gelendzhik would take an interested individual to the residence at Cape Idokopas, AKA Putin's palace, a $1.4 billion, 190,000-square-foot facility that was one of President Vladimir Putin's vacation homes. The 186-acre complex, with its spectacular views of the Black Sea, had, on occasion, been used by guests personally invited by Putin.

In addition to the mammoth house, the property included a guest house, a large greenhouse, a church, an ice palace, an amphitheater, a gas station, a helipad, and a 260-foot bridge tunnel. The sky above the property had been designated as a no-fly zone, and the perimeter of the property was heavily protected by the Russian FSB.

Annika Antonov had just passed the midway point of her ten-mile run; the last half was a steady incline. Her breaths were measured, her pace steady. The burn in her legs sent a welcome signal to her brain—that she was running at a record pace. Her strength and stamina were at their best. She didn't smile, but the gleam in her eyes said it all. Off to her left, a spectacular view of the sparkling Black Sea spread wide and far into the distance.

With just two hundred yards to go, Annika began a hard sprint, pushing herself. Always pushing for better, faster, stronger. As she approached the south entrance and watched the palace gates open, she flashed past the armed security team, slowed to a jog, then walked a bit before coming to a stop. The former champion pole vaulter leaned against a nearby wall to stretch the backs of her legs.

Roman Mirov stood several feet ahead beneath the sage-green awning, feet planted wide apart, arms crossed, watching her like a running coach might. When she glanced up at him, he looked at his watch, set to the stopwatch setting, then smiled as he called out: "49:11, excellent!"

Annika was surprised to see him, but, disappointed in her time, she shook her head. "Shit, I thought I'd be under forty-eight."

Roman smiled as he approached her, offering his fist for a bump. After Annika obliged, he picked a large bottle of water off the black marble table to his right and handed it to her. His eyes drew up and down her body with a gleam of admiration. "Annika, you look wonderful. You've made excellent progress. Think back to when you first got here. The doctors were questioning if you would recover."

Annika had uncapped the water and been gulping it down, but after Roman's reflection of that past…incident…she stopped drinking. After a few seconds, she placed her bottle on the ground next to her foot, looked at Roman, and smiled. "Thanks, and it's good to see you." With hands on her hips, she leaned from side to side, continuing her stretching, then paused. She pulled her sweatshirt over her head, fingers lightly touching the scar on her abdomen, where just eight months before, a bullet had almost ended her life. She briefly thought back to that snowy night in Washington when she escaped the White House and then blacked out from the sudden and instant pain.

Thankfully, she was saved when her driver carried her to safety and got her on a predawn flight bound for Mother Russia.

Suddenly snapping back to present time, she started stretching again. "Roman, it's been weeks since you were last here."

Roman raised an eyebrow. "Annika, it's been more than six months!"

Annika stopped stretching and stared at him. "Wow, you're right. So, what brings you here? I don't believe Putin is due anytime soon."

"We'll discuss over lunch. The chef will serve us in the guest house courtyard in an hour. Go shower. I've got some calls to make." Annika nodded, and Roman gave her half a wave as he walked off.

• • •

Annika, looking relaxed in jeans and an oversized University of Maryland hoodie, sat at the outdoor table sipping a vitamin drink. Roman joined and took the closest chair to hers.

A butler in a crisp, white shirt, black pants, and a black bowtie stepped up and asked if there would be any drinks.

Roman answered before Annika could. "I'll have a large Mamont vodka. She's in training, so bring her water."

Annika laughed. "Make that a Baltika pale lager. Beer is part of my training!"

Twenty feet away, the chef, working speedily, chest and head visible above the smoking grill attached to his small mobile kitchen, looked up and asked, "Are we ready?"

Annika and Roman, glancing over in response to the chef, both responded in unison, "Yes!" They looked at each other and chuckled.

The chef placed the food on solid stone plates and nodded to the butler, who immediately brought the plates to the table.

Annika glanced up from her food to address the chef. "This looks wonderful. What have we here?"

The chef, a man in his thirties with sharp cheekbones and dark hair and eyes, answered in a clipped, professional tone, "Walnut-stuffed black sea bass, and since you two are such special guests, my best beluga caviar salad."

The butler served their drinks and asked if everything was fine, to which Annika politely nodded and thanked him.

Roman faced Annika and smiled as they began to eat. "You look good with dark hair, and your tan makes you look most healthy."

"Yes, I think, before, when I was a pale blonde, it made me look too Eastern European."

Roman continued his intense, blatant stare. "How are the French lessons?"

"Manifique!" Annika switched from perfect French to Russian as she went on. "Language and writing are mastered. My next lesson is tonight, and we're focusing on European and international law."

Roman absorbed that with a nod. "Of course, and by the way, for the new you, international law is your major from the Sorbonne, and from this point forward, I want you to speak in English with a French accent."

Annika smiled, and then said in English with a thick French lilt, "But of course!"

Roman's lips shadowed a smile. "We can review your newly updated dossier after lunch."

They ate in silence for a few minutes. Roman, with his mouth full, raised his eyes to the butler, who stood absolutely still, gazing at the couple from fifteen feet away, then pointed to his glass and looked to Annika, who shook her head no to another beer.

"I cannot believe I've been here eight months," Annika commented, glancing at her surroundings. Lavish but solitary. Cold.

Roman's eyes again swept her. "Any side effects?"

"None at all. Fortunately, that bastard, Jonathan Cartwright, didn't use hollow points. The bullet went clear through me, not hitting any bones or vital organs—all of which you know since you have already read my medical reports." Annika put her fork down. "So, Roman... It's always good to see you, but tell me, what's the real purpose of this visit?"

Roman's drink arrived. He wiped his mouth with his napkin, then took a long pull from his vodka mug, holding and admiring the thick-cut glass before his gaze met Annika's. "Your recuperation is complete. We need you back in Washington."

Annika nodded. "I'm so pleased to hear this. I was dreading that my next assignment might require me to spend years in Moscow. So, why am I needed back in Washington?"

Roman again admired his glass. "Let's just say, we had an opening. The agent that took your place, Victor Orloff, miserably failed his most recent assignment. He has now been assigned to Vladimir."

Annika stared ahead in thought for a few seconds, then snapped her gaze at Roman. "Vladimir? What's in Vla... Oh my God, Vladimir Central, the maximum-security prison?!"

Roman's only response was to take another swallow from his drink.

• • •

After lunch, the two moved inside the guest house, pulling out two chairs on either side of the dining room table and then settling directly across from one another. Roman opened his briefcase, took out several folders, and laid them out. He then broke the silence: "Show me your hands."

Annika held out both hands, palms up.

Roman reached across the table and held her hands in his. After deeply massaging her palms and fingertips for several seconds with his thumbs, he asked, "Any discomfort?"

"None at all. When they first did the procedure about six months ago, my hands hurt a lot. But eventually, the pain eased. Now…it's amazing. No pain or sensitivity at all."

"Excellent. We've really become advanced in the science of fingerprint transplants. The woman we got

them from was a fruit picker in our chernozem region."
Roman's gaze became intense and probing. "Your
brown eyes are nice, very convincing."

"Yes, I went from a rail-thin blonde with blue eyes
to dark brown hair and brown eyes. Oh, and then
there's the twenty-five pounds of added muscle! So,
basically…" Her lips turned up in a smile. "…I've gone
from a pole vaulter to a powerlifter!"

"Precisely! And let's not forget the success of your
last assignment, and how it earned you the promotion
to major."

Annika's smile broadened. "From lowly corporal to
major in one of the fastest Russian military promotion
cycles in history."

The pride was clear on Roman's face. "You earned
it! And now, let's get into the details of the new you."
Roman reached for and opened a folder, pulling out a
page and handing it to Annika. "Your new dossier."

Annika read from the sheet: "Sylvie Bardot, single,
aged thirty." She grinned. "Thank you for making me
two years younger!"

Roman smiled and waved her on. "Keep reading."

Annika obliged. "Sylvie Bardot, born in Limoges, France. Moved to Paris at age seventeen, attended the Sorbonne for five years, earned a post-graduate law degree with a concentration in international law. Started as a paralegal and translator in the Paris offices of Winthrow & Strawn LLP. After five years, promoted to legal counsel, and now has been approved to participate in an exchange program to work six months at the Rayburn House Office Building in Washington DC, for the House Ways and Means Committee."

Roman leaned back in his chair. "Starting early tomorrow morning, we will have experts meeting with you to get you up to speed on every aspect of your dossier. We've already established electronic records to validate your background, education, and employment. We have agents in place that will serve as references and vouch for you. And finally, we have strategic assets, or 'friends,' in the US that are providing outstanding character references. You will leave for Washington next week and report to your office on Capitol Hill for your US Congress staff orientation."

Chapter 6

Monday, November 2
Paris, Virginia

Jonathan looked at his watch. It was 7:30 a.m., about twenty minutes until sunrise, light enough for him to get started, he figured. He carried a fresh cup of coffee into the bedroom, where he found his wife, Tina, sitting up in bed checking her iPhone.

"Good morning, beautiful." With a warm smile, Jonathan placed the coffee on the bedside table next to her and leaned in, planting a kiss on her smooth forehead.

Tina, with her short blonde hair, five-foot-two and tipping the scale at just over one hundred pounds, looked younger than her sixty-three years. She yawned as she stretched her arms. Sounding sleepy she said, "Good morning. I'm so groggy. These fall mornings make it too easy to sleep in."

Jonathan straightened. "Okay, well, I'm outta here. Have a great day—love you."

Tina, now holding her coffee with two hands, looked up. "I love you. Be safe."

Jonathan Cartwright was sixty-seven, tall and thin with broad shoulders. A good-looking man, his neatly cut, blond medium-length hair was starting to gray. He was an avid cyclist which kept him in great shape. He earned his undergrad, MS, JD, and PhD all from the University of Michigan and spent a long career in the government, starting with the FBI, then moving into the NSA (National Security Agency) for many years. Now, he was employed with the Department of Justice. For the past eight months, Jonathan had been heading up the investigation into the assassination of former President John Blake. Jonathan's retirement from the federal government had been fabricated shortly after the president's death, thus ensuring he could work in secrecy. His office was at the secluded Mount Weather government facility.

The Mount Weather Emergency Operations Center, a secure, government command facility located at the northern end of the Blue Ridge Mountains in a remote area near Paris, Virginia, sat on 434 acres. It was a sprawling compound that contained several buildings and included an underground area that measured over six hundred thousand square feet. Originally, Mount Weather opened its doors as a weather station in the late 1800s. During the 1920s, its purpose abruptly changed, becoming the summer White House for President Calvin Coolidge. In recent years, Mount Weather functioned as a Continuity of Government (COG) and Continuity of Operations Planning (COOP) site.

Jonathan exited the garage of his large, four-bedroom A-frame, nestled in the hills a mile south of Paris, Virginia. He stood in the driveway and did a quick 360 survey of his surrounding eighteen acres. The fall morning air was cool, and the fog had lifted enough for him to spot the deer at the end of his thousand-foot-long driveway. Moving back into the garage, he kicked off his slippers, put on his cycling shoes, helmet, and gloves, and briefly inspected his bicycle, a Giant TCR carbon fiber. Satisfied, he was ready to go.

The morning ride from his house to his office at Mount Weather was mostly uphill and took about an hour; his evening ride home, all downhill, could be covered in half the time.

At 8:25 a.m., Jonathan slowed to a stop at the main gate of Mount Weather, tapped his ID to the reader, entered his pin on the keypad, walked his bike another few feet, and then showed the same ID to a uniformed officer who opened the gate. Once inside the complex, Jonathan rode the additional half-mile to his building, where he had to scan his ID again for entrance and then wheel his bike in through the door until he reached another door, where he placed his cell phones in a locked box before proceeding to a door where a scanner read the palm of his hand. He also had to enter an eight-digit access code at that point. After all of that, the door opened, and Jonathan walked in, bike in tow.

He was now in a SCIF (Sensitive Compartmented Information Facility) space used by the Department of Justice, National Security Division. He walked the remaining ninety feet to his corner office, tapped his ID card to yet another reader, then placed his thumb onto a scanner, after which his office door opened. Finally, he stepped inside to his nice-sized office. A large conference table led to his desk, which was at the far end of the room. Two of the walls were adorned with

nicely framed photos of Tina at various travel destinations, while another wall contained an
electronic board. The last wall was dominated by a large window looking out to the parking lot and beyond to a stunning view of the Shenandoah valley. Jonathan grabbed a garment bag from the closet behind his desk, left his office, locked the door behind him, and then headed to the locker room to take a shower and change out of his cycling gear.

. . .

A few minutes before 11 a.m., Jonathan received a call from Mount Weather Security: "Mr. Cartwright, we have your appointment, Frank Osborne, here to see you. He's already been processed through security. We can bring him over to you now if convenient."

"Absolutely," Jonathan agreed, leaning forward in his chair, phone in one hand and riffling through a few papers on his desk with the other. "And thanks, I'll meet him in front of my building."

Frank Osborne, age forty-nine, twice married and twice divorced, had earned his undergrad and law degree from the University of Virginia. He had worked his way up from the Secret Service Uniformed Division to lead agent, then he moved on to the Department of Justice, where he served as a US attorney. After spending some time on Wall Street, where he became a very successful investor, he moved to K Street and set up his law practice. Frank's net worth was among the highest in Washington, DC. Physically, he was overweight, but his appearance was greatly enhanced by his tailored suits and designer shoes. Thanks to a good hairdresser, Frank's hair was always dark brown and his full beard nicely trimmed. Frank was well known for his wit and sense of humor, he was an exceptional orator and champion debater, often quoting Lincoln, Churchill, or Shakespeare to make his point.

Early into the assassination investigation, Frank had worked endless hours assisting with Jonathan's efforts, for which Jonathan was eternally grateful.

Jonathan welcomed Frank with a handshake, then a hug and a grin, and brought him to his office and shut the door.

Jonathan pointed to the chair facing his desk. "Have a seat. I guess sailing across the Atlantic has been good for you. You look tanned, rested, and ready." His grin widened. "And I can tell you've lost weight!"

Frank grinned back, clearly pleased that Jonathan had noticed. "Yes, thirty-five pounds! Just twenty more to go, and I'll make my goal."

"Ah, man, that's great." Jonathan moved back to his desk and sank into his chair. "Good for you."

Frank took a seat. "Thanks. It's been—what? Six or eight months since I last saw you. How are you, and more importantly, how goes the investigation?"

"Well, I've been here since March. You were last here in April. So, it's been ongoing for seven months. You still have your clearance. You didn't do anything stupid in France, did you?"

Frank laughed. "No, I'm too old to do anything to jeopardize my clearance."

Jonathan nodded. "Well, you never would have made it into Mount Weather if there was anything that showed up. However, let me confirm you're still at the highest security level." He made an apologetic face.

"Sorry, but I'm sure you can understand, I must follow procedures. Heck, I wrote them!"

Frank lifted a shoulder in nonchalant acceptance, and Jonathan picked up his phone and pressed a button. After that, he faced his desk computer and tapped a few keys, then spoke into his phone: "This is Jonathan Cartwright. I need for you to verify a clearance: Frank Xavier Osborne, DOB 1-8-1974, Manhattan, New York." Jonathan fell silent, listening to the woman on the other end of the line running through instructions in a monotone voice, then said, "Yes, I'll have him do that right now. Hold on." His eyes flashed to Frank. "We need a thumb scan." Jonathan pointed to a fingerprint reader on his computer keyboard.

Frank got up and walked around to where he could place his thumb on the scanner. The green light indicated the scan had been read successfully.

Jonathan nodded. "Thanks, have a seat." He readdressed the woman on the phone: "Okay, what do we have?" After a few seconds, he added, "Yankee White, correct? Good. Please send me the non-disclosure agreement [NDA] for Frank to sign—I'm reading him back into the Blake assassination file.

Okay, standing by, thank you." Jonathan hung up, then looked at Frank. "We're good. Well, technically, you're good. You still have your top-secret SCI clearance. Once I read you in, you'll sign the NDA. Then we can talk."

One side of Frank's mouth quirked up. "Hey, before we start, what's the latest on the speaker?"

Jonathan shook his head. "Yeah, crazy story! Thankfully, the worst thing that happened was, when her security detail jumped on her to cover her, they broke her ankle in two places. I'm told she's mad as a hornet!"

Frank rubbed his chin. "Wow, the broken ankle hasn't made the news."

"No, not yet, but it will. I'm not directly involved with that case but can share with you the early details that the sniper was a local, unemployed loner who was a Vietnam vet suffering from post-traumatic stress disorder."

Frank stopped rubbing his chin, hand dropping into his lap. "Wow... So sad. Okay, please fill me in on your report."

Jonathan read Frank into the case, had him sign the paperwork, then began. "We're so close to nailing her!" Jonathan typed a few more commands into his computer, which resulted in an outline being displayed on the large, electronic board on his wall. "Let's sit at the conference table and I'll drive the presentation from there."

The two men took seats next to each other facing the large screen, and Jonathan pulled out a keyboard and started the presentation. "My investigation focused on the numerous touchpoints between President Elizabeth Gentry and Russian leadership. The evidence proves our initial theory—the one you helped me with. Elizabeth Gentry and her chief of staff, Wendy Wolf, began a relationship with the Russians when Gentry was a Navy pilot twenty years ago. As you recall, she was involved in the project for the F-35a stealth fighter. We now have empirical evidence that she facilitated the Russians in obtaining key classified components to the design plans for that aircraft. Then, as a quid pro quo, the Russians committed to getting Gentry elected to Congress."

Jonathan moved to his mini fridge as Frank continued to study the board. After grabbing two bottles of water, he headed back to the conference table and handed a bottle to Frank. Frank murmured a "thanks," obviously processing the information Jonathan provided.

Jonathan opened his bottle, took an absentminded sip, and sat down. "Once Gentry was elected to Congress, her meteoritic rise in politics was mostly due to her charisma and ability to persuade and attract voters."

Frank cocked his head. "We always agreed the woman is a rock star, drop-dead gorgeous, a young-looking Demi Moore, highly cerebral, great orator… And devious as hell." He rolled his eyes. "What's not to like?"

"We can now prove that there was a close relationship between President Gentry and Russian leadership, specifically with Russian Oligarch Roman Mirov, who has ties to Vladimir Putin. And all Mirov's activities were at the direction of Putin and the Kremlin." Jonathan swiveled his head, eyes back on the board. "My report diagrams the money trail starting from Gentry's days in the Navy."

"Right. Didn't Roman Mirov contribute to all of her campaigns?"

"Ah, yes!" Jonathan gave a nod. "Mirov contributed over a million dollars to a political action committee [PAC] for each of Elizabeth Gentry's three congressional campaigns and another $900,000 to the Blake-Gentry PAC for president. And get this—less than one week after President Blake's assassination, he met with Gentry at the White House. Mirov and his wife were overnight guests!" Jonathan smirked. "The next day, he contributed five million dollars to Elizabeth Gentry's new presidential PAC!"

Frank's eyes bulged. "Holy shit! So, obviously, tons of ethics violations… But how do you prove criminal activity, specifically, President Gentry's involvement in the assassination of President Blake?"

Jonathan took a long breath. "Well, let's step back and look at why the Russians thought they'd be better without President Blake. Years ago, then-Senator Blake was renowned for his disdain of Russia and communism. Even held several public hearings on Russian corruption. Clearly, Russian leadership saw Blake as the biggest threat to their plans for world domination. For years, the Russians would have liked nothing better than to eliminate Blake. And once it was leaked that President Blake had formed a coalition with plans to liberate Crimea and Syria, the Russians must have felt they had no choice but to move forward, and use their foreign service agents to eliminate Blake."

Jonathan's eyes hardened, his mind flashing back to the former president...and his tragic murder. "The Russians knew they could successfully leverage their relationship with Vice President Elizabeth Gentry. We now have proof that, over the past several months, Gentry used a variety of burner phones for her communications with the Russians. With help from our friends at the NSA and CIA, plus engineers from AT&T and Verizon, we've been able to recover close to 75 percent of Gentry's burner phone text conversations." Jonathan tapped a knuckle on the tabletop. "We've also got records of the times and dates for all voice conversations and are working out the actual text of those conversations as we speak."

With nervous energy, Jonathan stood and headed to the window, staring outside as if itching to lead the charge against Gentry personally. "We recently were able to get sworn affidavits from two White House butlers who overheard Oligarch Roman Mirov and President Elizabeth Gentry's conversation in the White House private residence shortly after Blake's assassination, during which Gentry congratulated Mirov for 'masterfully' orchestrating the change in power."

Jonathan advanced to the final slide in his deck. "We have proof beyond any reasonable doubt that President Elizabeth Gentry was a key participant in collusion with the Russians in the assassination of President Blake. We know Elizabeth Gentry, through Roman Mirov, facilitated FSB Agent Annika Antonov's access to the White House, which ended with my shooting Antonov during her escape with her lover during that freak March blizzard." Jonathan's eyes again clouded as he briefly revisited that emotionally charged memory. "We believe Antonov is dead, but Roman Mirov is still around, and we need to find him." Jonathan faced Frank. "I sent my draft of the investigation to the attorney general [AG] yesterday."

Chapter 7

Monday, November 2
The White House

It was a few minutes past 5 p.m. The president was enjoying a scotch as she sat in the West Sitting Hall of the White House private residence. After a long time spent in contemplative silence, she abruptly picked up the nearby phone, waited for the administration operator to answer, and then said, "Yes, get me the attorney general."

A moment later, the operator responded with, "On the line, Madam President."

Barely waiting for the AG to voice a greeting, Gentry demanded, "Edward, how fast can you get over here?"

Edward quickly answered, "I can be there in less than fifteen minutes."

"Get here in ten. See you then." She hung up.

Gentry then pressed the buzzer for the butler. Less than five seconds later, Nathan, an older man wearing a black suit and bowtie, walked in from the second-floor pantry.

Gentry stared up at him. "Nathan, I want you to gather all the butlers for a meeting with me at 6 p.m."

Nathan nodded. "Yes, ma'am. I'm not sure if all of them are available, but I'll check."

Gentry's eyes were as hard and cold as marbles. "I didn't ask if they were available. I expect all the butlers that want to continue working at the White House to be here in the West Sitting Hall at 6 p.m. sharp. Now go and make it happen. You're dismissed."

Nathan, already having grown used to the new president's demanding nature, agreed and turned to follow her orders.

President Gentry again picked up the phone from the end table, waited a few seconds, then barked into the receiver, "Get me the chef." She put it back on the cradle and stared into space, nursing her drink. Moments later, it rang, and she answered it impatiently.

As soon as the operator reported that the chef was on the line, Gentry blurted out instructions.

"Chef, I'll have a mixed salad and a bowl of that wonderful lentil soup you make. Have the butlers serve it to me in the West Sitting Hall at 7 p.m." She was off the phone and back to staring intensely into space before the chef could reply.

The phone on the end table rang. Gentry answered, listened to the caller, and said: "Yes, I'm expecting him. Send him up." She hung up.

Attorney General Edward Stanton got off the elevator on the second floor and slowly walked into the West Sitting Hall. Stanton was a tall man in his fifties, but he looked older, his hair gray, and his face lined with wrinkles.

Gentry waved her perfectly manicured fingers at the nearest chair. "Edward, have a seat. We need to talk."

The attorney general sat in an oversized chair five feet from the couch, facing Gentry. He waited in silence for her to get to the reason for his rushed visit.

"Edward, I understand that you have the draft of the Blake assassination investigation. Have you read it?"

Edward, caught off-guard, blinked twice before answering. "Uh, Madam President, I have to say, it's highly irregular that you would know that I have the draft…and are asking if I read it."

She lowered her glass, staring daggers at the AG. "Ed, cut the bullshit. We both know what can happen to you if you try and play games with me. I would hate for your wife, Belinda, and the press to learn that you're sleeping with your chief of staff, and even worse, if they discovered how you benefitted from insider trading on that $50 million stock deal." Her lips began to quirk up, though her delight seemed lost beneath the calculating gleam in her eyes. "And finally, *Eddie*, no one really needs to know the truth about you and Jerry Epstein, do they…?" She smiled sweetly. "Do I have your full attention now?"

The attorney general looked down, a faint sheen of sweat making his forehead glossy as he nodded a slow yes.

Gentry dropped the saccharine-sweet smile. "I'm glad you understand me. Now, I need your guarantee that this so-called assassination report will never see the light of day. Can I count on you for this, or do I need to get someone else involved?"

Edward straightened in his chair, smoothing his tie nervously. "Yes. I have the report and I will lose it. You can count on me."

She nodded curtly. "Thank you, Edward, I appreciate your continued dedication. You are a true patriot. Be sure and let me know if you encounter any hiccups." President Gentry stood. "Thank you for coming on such short notice."

The attorney general stood without a word, turned toward the elevator, and left with hurried steps.

President Gentry, face neutral, glanced absently at her nearly empty drink before pressing the button for the butler. Immediately, Nathan reappeared in the West Sitting Hall.

Gentry glanced over at him. "It's almost six, Nathan," she pointed out like a mother slowly losing her patience with a young child. "Who's here?"

Nathan answered readily, "Six of the seven butlers are here. The last one should be arriving any minute."

"You've got ten minutes. Bring them all in at six—and get me a cup of coffee."

"Right away, ma'am." Nathan headed back to the pantry.

. . .

Nathan entered the West Sitting Hall carrying a tray and coffee for the president, followed by six butlers walking in lockstep, soldier-style. Nathan placed the tray on the coffee table in front of the president and waited with unending patience for her next command.

Without making eye contact with any of the men, Gentry swept a hand toward the furniture in front of her. "Gentlemen, take a seat."

Each butler silently took a chair in the vast room.

Gentry began, "Throughout the history of the White House Executive Residence, the staff have always been the most dedicated, reliable, and trusted individuals. Never in its history has there been a confirmed breach of trust, nor has there ever been anything shared by the staff that would embarrass the first family. The residence staff is privy to the most intimate details, not just family privacy but also items of national security. I applaud all the staff, especially the butlers."

President Gentry took an unhurried sip of her coffee, then continued, "It has come to my attention that two butlers recently were coerced into signing affidavits regarding details of a conversation I may have had. I say *coerced…*" The word seemed strained as it passed her lips. "…because I cannot believe any butler would voluntarily take such action. I know which two of you did this." She seemed to hesitate. "I did not want to take any personnel action against those two individuals because I believe this was not an action that you took on your own, and I also wanted all seven of you to hear this from me."

Gentry gave a stern look at each of the men, then added, "I want to emphasize that none of you should ever assume, by hearing a portion of a conversation, that you fully understand the context or reason for such an exchange. In other words, gentlemen, there is a lot more going on in the background than meets the eye. I have taken an oath to solemnly swear to faithfully execute the Office of the President of the United States, and to the best of my ability, preserve, protect, and defend the Constitution. Gentlemen, understand, any and all the actions I take are for the best of the country." The president paused. "Are there any questions or comments?"

The butlers all stared at the president with no comment and without any hint of emotion.

Gentry seemed satisfied. "Good. I expect the two butlers that signed affidavits to immediately reach out to the person who contacted them and withdraw their statements. Thank you, gentlemen, that will be all."

Chapter 8

Monday, November 2
Mount Weather, Virginia

It was the end of a long day; Jonathan glanced at his watch. Still a half hour of daylight left, which was just enough for him to get home.

With his bike gear on, he walked out of his building. Once outdoors, alone with his bike, he immediately felt calm and relaxed. The autumn air was crisp and the fall foliage stunning. He enjoyed his rides home, which were mostly downhill. As soon as he scanned his ID at the exit gate, it opened, and away he went, heading south on Blue Ridge Mountain Road.

A mile and a half into his eight-mile ride, Jonathan was startled by the sound of a vehicle approaching from the rear. He rarely encountered vehicles on this road. Frowning, Jonathan slowed and moved as far right as possible.

He heard a sharp pop, immediately followed by an excruciating pain in his left leg. Jonathan looked down to see his thigh bleeding. Instinctively, his left hand moved toward the injury, causing his bike to veer left. He glanced back at the Ford F-150 bearing down on him, and Jonathan grabbed at his brakes—right before he was propelled through the sky.

He and his bike flew high over the guardrail and into the abyss of the valley below.

Chapter 9

Wednesday, November 4
George Washington Hospital, Washington, DC

Jonathan opened his eyes. For an instant, the world seemed blurry; he couldn't focus. Then the pain in his legs and shoulder overcame his senses, and he blacked out.

Several minutes later, he again awoke—this time to a soft caress on his face. He opened his eyes to see his wife gazing down at him with concern. He tried to speak, but no words would come.

Tina's face brightened. "Honey, it's okay. You're in George Washington University Hospital. The best doctors and specialists are here taking care of you."

Jonathan swallowed; his tongue felt like it was coated in sand, and his throat burned. "The pain," he whispered hoarsely. "Really bad."

Tina reached for and pressed the IV button to administer more painkillers. "There, that should help," she murmured softly.

Moments later, Jonathan felt a rush of relief flow through him, though the pain remained an unwelcome companion in the background. "Why am I here? What happened?"

Tina answered, "You were in a bike accident. When it got to be after sunset, and you weren't home, I called Mount Weather Security. The operator said you had exited at 18:10. After I told them you didn't make it back to the house, they immediately started a search. They found you just after midnight in a valley several hundred feet beneath the road."

Jonathan winced—even that seemed to hurt. "I don't remember anything. Why am I here?"

Before Tina could respond, they were interrupted by a doctor who glided into the room.

"Hello, I am Dr. Howard, the attending physician here at GW. Nice to see you awake." Howard, a forty-year-old African American, was wearing a white lab coat. He checked some readings, then asked Jonathan how he felt.

Jonathan, still trying to push through the fog that lingered in his mind, slowly replied: "I hurt all over... My legs, my shoulder, and my head is pounding."

"You are being treated for multiple injuries," the doctor informed him. "Your left clavicle is fractured, which would account for the pain in your shoulder. You also have a fracture in your right femur, which you had surgery for when you arrived. You most likely sustained a closed head injury. That means you may be suffering from a concussion. Now that you're awake, we will run a full examination. And finally, you have a gunshot wound in your left thigh."

Jonathan's bleary eyes shot fully open. "What the hell—a gunshot?!"

Dr. Howard frowned. "Yes, I'm afraid so, and given your position with the government, well... There are a lot of people that I have been holding off that need to talk to you."

Jonathan blinked a few times. "How long have I been here?"

"Two days," responded the doctor.

. . .

Attorney General Edward Stanton's security detail entered Jonathan's hospital room, followed by Edward himself, who looked at Tina, flashed a smile, and said, "Thanks for calling me." He then faced Jonathan. "Tina has been providing me updates. I waited until you were conscious to visit. How are you doing?"

Jonathan offered a wan smile of his own. "Ed, thanks for coming. I'm doing okay, I guess. Still in a lot of pain and a bit bewildered.... I just don't remember what happened."

The attorney general turned to the head of his security detail and asked him and his team to leave the room. He then looked at Tina with an apologetic expression. "I'm sorry, but I really need to speak to your husband in private."

Tina responded, "Of course, understood." She gently squeezed Jonathan's arm. "Hon, I'm going to grab a late lunch. I'll be back in a half hour or so."

Jonathan grasped her hand as she started to leave and mouthed, *I love you.* Tina gave a warm smile and turned away.

Jonathan waited until she had closed the door behind her. "Okay, Ed, what do we know?"

"You were shot by an M4," the attorney general said bluntly.

Jonathan furrowed his brow. "Huh? Military-grade?"

"Yes. Mount Weather surveillance video shows at least two shots were fired from a Ford F-150 by a masked man in the passenger seat. The truck then hit the rear of your bike, which caused you to go airborne and over the guardrail into the valley below. The truck then stopped, and two masked men in fatigues got out, looked over the guardrail for a few seconds, and, likely satisfied you were dead, left in a hurry. The final video shows them making a left onto Route 50, headed toward DC. We're working with Virginia State Police to get all traffic videos in the area, and by the way, the truck had its license plates covered."

Jonathan rubbed his face. "My God, who even knew I was at Mount Weather?"

The attorney general slid the lone chair in the hospital room closer to Jonathan's bed, sat down, and leaned forward, meeting Jonathan's gaze intensely. "We're looking into that, gathering intel on the Russians. We have not yet detected any communications chatter." He straightened. "By the way, you're in good company—the Speaker of the House is recuperating just down the hall."

Jonathan rolled his eyes. "Oh, great, I'm going to need security. Congress is not good at keeping secrets. It won't be long before the press reports that I am here."

The side of Edward's mouth turned up. "Already in place. As soon as Tina called me, I assigned FBI and DC Metropolitan Police to round-the-clock protection. I also have the FBI outside of your house."

Jonathan smiled. "Thanks. You know, some things are starting to come back to me. I remember seeing...the F150 was red!"

Edward nodded encouragingly. "Yes, it was. Good, and let me know as you remember things. I'm going to head back to the office and will visit again soon. In the meantime, don't hesitate to call me directly." He stood to leave.

"Thanks so much." Jonathan shifted, settling into his bed, lids growing heavy again. Then his eyes flashed to Edward. "Oh! Any initial thoughts on my report?"

With a quizzical look, the attorney general stared at Jonathan. "What are you talking about?"

"My draft of the assassination report! I sent it, via JWICS1! Sunday night."

---

1 Joint Worldwide Intelligence Communication System, United States Department of Defense's secure intranet system that houses top-secret and sensitive compartmented information.

Edward frowned, his shoulders lifting in a faint shrug. "Nope, never saw it."

Chapter 10

Thursday, November 5
Dulles Airport, Virginia

Annika Antonov—currently known as Sylvie Bardot—exited her Air France flight and headed to immigrations. She looked attractive and stylish in her black denim jeans, cognac-colored Azura lambskin jacket, chic white t-shirt, and goatskin leather ankle boots that perfectly matched her jacket. She wheeled her carry-on behind her; her backpack was slung over her shoulder. Several trunks had already been shipped to her soon-to-be home, an apartment on Capitol Hill. At the moment, she found herself standing in a long line to be checked by US Customs and Border Protection.

After a fifteen-minute wait, she stepped up to the window and presented her French passport and green card with a bright smile. The US Customs and Border Protection officer, unmoved by her fetching expression, sternly asked for her full name and date of birth.

In perfect English, but with just a hint of a French accent, she gave her answer: "Sylvie Bergier Bardot, birthday: October 4, 1993."

The officer's face seemed molded from granite. "Is your travel for business or pleasure?"

Sylvie's engaging, warm smile didn't falter. "Mostly work, but I am hoping for a little pleasure as well…?"

The officer, unable to maintain his façade in the presence of such a beguiling woman, broke into a smile, then stamped her passport and handed it to her. "Enjoy your stay."

. . .

Sylvie paid the cab driver and got out, facing the building at 218 4th Street SE, her new address. The street was quiet and the fourth-floor, furnished apartment in a historic brownstone. She was looking forward to the next few days, during which she planned on setting up her apartment and maybe even taking in a museum or two. She was thrilled that her apartment was only a twelve-minute walk to the Rayburn House

Office Building, where she would report on Monday for orientation.

Things were going perfectly so far…

Chapter 11

Friday, November 6
George Washington Hospital, Washington, DC

Jonathan slowly awakened to the feeling that someone was staring at him. Gradually, he turned his head, then jumped a little. He would have done a double-take if moving were a little less painful. The Speaker of the House sat in a wheelchair right next to his bed! He grimaced, trying to tamp down the waves of pain created by his sudden movement as he squinted, struggling to make out the speaker in a blue medical frock, leg in a big white cast fully extended and held up by a leg extension on her wheelchair.

Speaker Suzanne Montgomery was looking straight at him. She raised an eyebrow in amusement. "Hello, bright eyes. I knew, if I waited long enough, you'd wake up."

Jonathan muttered, "Ah, hello, Madam Speaker."

"Jonathan, we met years ago when I was chair of the Intelligence Committee. I never forgot how impressed I was with your testimony. I'm so glad to see you're recovering—and how cool is it that we both ended up in the same hospital? I see it as some sort of divine intervention!"

Jonathan grew much more alert. "Yes, Madam Speaker, I remember my testimony as if it were yesterday."

Suzanne waved a hand. "Oh, Jonathan, call me Suzanne, please. No need for us to be formal. We're old friends."

Jonathan smiled amicably, even as he thought, *the only thing she got right is that we are old!* "Suzanne, how is your recovery going?"

She sighed. "I've got pins in my ankles. They want me to start therapy later this week. I told them no way, that I need to get back to the office. They said I would be here for at least two more weeks. I reminded them, the country is depending on me to be back on the Hill this week! But enough of that—there are more important things for us to discuss."

Jonathan rested his head against the pillow. "Fire away. I'm not going anywhere anytime soon."

Suzanne grinned. "I like your spirit, Jonathan. So, let's get down to it. I believe you and I have a mutual disdain for the person that currently resides at 1600 Pennsylvania Avenue."

Jonathan raised his eyebrow, listening quite intently now.

Chapter 12

Monday, November 9
US Capitol Complex, Washington, DC

Sylvie Bardot completed the rudimentary new employee orientation, thankful for her status as a six-month temporary employee. It meant she was excused from having to attend the most boring and mundane portions of the session. As she left the orientation room, she almost ran into Jennifer Largent.

"Hello, Sylvie," the woman greeted her in a rush. "I'm Jennifer Largent, the Speaker of the House's chief of staff. Welcome to the US Congress. We decided that rather than dump you into the Ways and Means Committee offices, you should tag along with me today to get a better idea on how things work around here. Then we'll discuss a special assignment the speaker has in mind for you. Follow me, as you'll soon learn time is always of the essence on Capitol Hill."

Sylvie, surprised, smiled widely. "Wow, this sounds wonderful, and thank you."

Jennifer gave her a look of caution. "Before you thank me, you should wait and see what we have in store for you. You came highly recommended to us. The speaker personally reviewed your resume and was so impressed, she selected you for a special assignment. You won't get to meet the speaker yet since she's still in the hospital, but she expects to be back in the office soon. And let me be very frank with you—your value is that you are a resource! Every office on Capitol Hill is extremely short-staffed, so when we see someone with an advanced degree and not tied to any one member of Congress, we use our powers in the speaker's office to borrow and best allocate that resource. The speaker is literally and figuratively the king of the Hill. Everyone in the House majority reports to her!"

Jennifer, falling silent, led Sylvie to the Architect of the Capitol's office.

The Architect of the Capitol (AOC), though a relatively unknown and small agency, housed two thousand employees responsible for the upkeep, maintenance, historic preservation, and facilities management for the US Capitol Building, all the Senate and House Office Buildings, the Library of Congress complex, and the Supreme Court Building. In total, the AOC was responsible for twenty-two buildings on 283 acres. AOC employees had more access to all facets of the Capitol Hill complex than any other entity in Washington. Though the agency was officially non-political, its head, known as the "Architect," registered through the American Institute of Architects and was appointed by the president and confirmed by the Senate for a ten-year term.

Jennifer and Sylvie entered the large, cavernous office area, well-hidden and one level down from the Capitol dome. They approached the receptionist, who was surprised and a bit intimidated to see the speaker's chief of staff.

Jennifer announced, "We're here to see the Architect. He's expecting us." Before the stunned receptionist could react, the large doors to the Architect's office opened, and out walked the man himself, Derek Monet, who greeted Jennifer with a warm smile.

Gregarious and handsome, Derek had been confirmed as the Architect of the Capitol five years earlier when only thirty-seven, thus becoming the youngest Architect in the history of the office. Derek had prospered in his position and was liked and trusted by staff and members of Congress on both sides of the aisle. The man managed to handle delicately one of the more difficult jobs in all of Washington: managing the assignments and rotations of the offices for all 435 House members and one hundred senators, a tremendous task that occurred every two years and was based on seniority and power. His close working relationships with various "well-connected" Hill individuals had provided him with some of the more coveted inside information in all of Washington.

Derek offered a smile. "Hello, Jennifer, always great to see you." His attention moved to the woman beside her. "And this must be Sylvie. Welcome to the Capitol." He shook Sylvie's hand, holding it within both of his. "We're here to help you succeed in achieving the goals of the speaker."

Sylvie, appearing a bit awestruck, smiled sheepishly. "Thank you for the warm welcome."

Derek motioned to the two of them. "Come into my office." Jennifer led the way, followed by Sylvie.

Once both women were inside, Derek quietly closed the door behind them. "Have a seat."

Jennifer and Sylvie settled onto a large leather sofa while Derek took a leather wing chair facing them.

"Would either of you like some coffee or tea?" he asked politely.

Sylvie waited for Jennifer to shake her head no, then followed suit.

Jennifer shifted in her seat. "Derek, as I mentioned on the phone, you know all too well the…let's call them 'challenges'…we are facing with the current staff shortages and staff allocations, etc." Derek nodded, and Jennifer continued, "The Government Accountability Office is on our back all the time. Already, this year, we've had to respond to four audits." She sneered. "And then, of course, the House minority leader and Senate majority leader have partnered in promising the American people that the Hill will cut the fat, so to speak, and eliminate Congressional staff by 30 percent before the end of the year! We need a place to hide Sylvie for a few days until the speaker is back." After a weighted pause, she added, "You mentioned you could handle it."

Derek straightened. "Absolutely, and as you know, I've done this a few times in the past for the speaker."

Jennifer's body seemed to visibly relax. "Thank you, Derek. The speaker knew you'd be able to help. Let me provide you with additional background, and Sylvie, consider this a more specific orientation." Sylvie nodded quickly, and then Jennifer continued, "Sylvie has a law degree in international law from the Sorbonne. She speaks several languages, and the speaker received the highest praise regarding her capabilities from some of the most important people in the country. Our background check revealed one of the most stellar employment records of anyone we've brought on, and so, the speaker is already working with Sylvie's law firm in France to convert Sylvie's six-month internship into a permanent employment position with us. The speaker wants to have Sylvie work on some emerging European trade agreements, with various Euro economies, and even possibly with Russia, if this damn war with Ukraine ever ends. Sylvie will need to have a private office equivalent to a director level. Can you handle that?"

Derek's smile was confident. "Absolutely. I have a couple of locations we can consider."

Chapter 13

Monday, November 9
George Washington Hospital, Washington, DC

Dr. Howard's eyes were focused on his iPad as he walked into Jonathan's room. He finally looked up to see Jonathan seated in his bed, his wife Tina standing beside him. Jonathan's left arm was in a sling, and the cast on his left leg jutted out from under the sheet.

Dr. Howard greeted them with a jovial, "Hello, Cartwrights. Mr. Cartwright, how are you feeling?"

Jonathan glanced down at himself. "I still have considerable pain in my legs and shoulder—not much improvement from yesterday."

Dr. Howard nodded sympathetically. "I'm afraid it will be another day or so before you start to feel better. I can increase your meds to make you more comfortable..."

"That won't be necessary," answered Jonathan. "Thank you."

Tina spoke up. "Dr. Howard, my husband feels he needs to remain as alert as possible in order to do his work."

"Understood." The doctor gave Jonathan a serious look. "Mr. Cartwright, just to manage expectations, the earliest you may be leaving here will be two weeks—maybe longer—then you will require outpatient physical therapy for up to forty-five days and then several more follow-up visits. I suggest you plan on being here for a while." The doctor moved to the bed and probed Jonathan's upper arm and collarbone area. "The swelling has reduced," he commented. "That's good." He stood back. "Let me look at your legs."

Jonathan pulled back his sheet to reveal a large cast on his right leg and bandages on his left thigh.

Dr. Howard ignored the cast and slowly removed the bandages. "This is doing well, but I want to leave it exposed for a while. The nurse will redress it." He added, "All your vitals are looking good. Do you have any questions?"

Jonathan had an immediate one on his mind, which he voiced: "How soon before I can use a wheelchair?"

"Soon," the doctor promised. "Maybe in a couple of days. We'll see."

Jonathan nodded, and Tina said, "Thank you, Doctor."

The doctor moved to exit the room but had to abruptly step aside to allow four men in.

Jonathan smiled in disbelief. "Oh, my god! I can't believe it. Who let you guys in here?!"

Attorney Frank Osborne was the first to speak. "We were worried about you, so I got the posse together so we could come see you."

Jonathan looked on, pleased but surprised beyond words as Bartholomew Winston, Brent Williams, and Greg Leidner followed Frank toward the bed.

Jonathan felt like his life was passing before his eyes.

Bartholomew, known to all as Winston, was seventy-six and aging gracefully. He had spent fifty-one years in the White House serving as the chief usher, managing the operations of the White House for ten US presidents until his retirement four months earlier. He spoke with a deep inflection and a slight southern dialect, indicative of his rural North Carolina roots, where he earned his bachelor's degree from Winston-Salem State University. Immediately after college, Winston had joined the Marines, going on to become a decorated Vietnam War vet after two tours in combat. Winston was a classic sort of man who always stood tall and rigid as if at attention. During his White House years, he had been conservatively stylish with his well-fitted suits, wearing a fedora when outdoors. He had a remarkable resemblance to Morgan Freeman; people often confused him with the famous actor. His wife, Connie, had been tragically killed in a car accident a couple of years earlier, and subsequently he focused on nothing but his work, sleeping most nights at the White House until his retirement last August.

Brent Williams stood at Winston's side, gazing down at Jonathan. A former assistant White House usher, Brent had left the White House after being labeled a temporary suspect in the assassination of former President John Blake. Completely exonerated, he had ended up being a valuable resource for the Blake assassination investigation.

Greg Leidner grinned at Jonathan, who couldn't help but grin back. The former Secret Service agent had also been instrumental in assisting with the investigation into the assassination.

Tina stepped forward and hugged each of the men, then the four moved close and gingerly shook Jonathan's hand.

"Winston and Greg, weren't you guys in California?" inquired Jonathan.

Winston responded first with a smile. "I was in Philadelphia visiting a friend." The expression faltered as his eyes swept Jonathan's injuries. "Frank called to fill me in, and I was here in just a couple of hours."

Greg chimed in, "I was already here visiting with Brent."

Brent pointed out, "Don't forget, you've been here for a few days already. We've been waiting for the doctors to allow us to see you."

Jonathan nodded. "How've you all been? Winston, we last talked several weeks ago. How are the twin grandbabies?"

Winston beamed. "They're wonderful. Just a couple of months old and beyond adorable!"

Jonathan smiled. "And how are you and the former first lady getting along?"

This brought a big smile to Winston. "Beverly and I are well. She visits me in San Diego often. As a matter of fact, the reason I was back east in Philadelphia was to see her. Just six weeks ago, we enjoyed a Rhine River cruise, and now we just began planning for a cruise in the Antarctic!"

"Fabulous!" Jonathan's eyes traveled to the other two men. "Brent and Greg, what's new?"

"Six more months to complete my PhD." Brent theatrically pretended to wipe sweat off his forehead. "Then, hopefully, take a break before working."

Greg offered, "Living on the West Coast is great, and providing security to the rich and famous is never dull."

Jonathan nodded. "Excellent, guys. I've missed you all, more than you know."

Frank got serious. "Jonathan, I cannot believe I saw you the day of your accident, and that was just one week ago. I'm so sorry this happened to you. Oh, by the way, I was able to confirm, all of us still have our clearances, and we all want to help you through whatever is going on here."

Winston stepped forward. "That's right. It'll be just like last March after President Blake's assassination when we all worked together. We're here to help."

Tina, seeing this as an opportune time to leave the men to themselves, stood, kissed Jonathan on the cheek, and said, "Looks like you're in good hands. I'm going to head home. I'll return first thing in the morning."

Jonathan smiled up at her. "Okay, love. You're being driven by the FBI, right?"

"Yes, of course." She gave him a reassuring nod. "Two agents, and there are also agents at the house. I'll be fine." She turned and blew kisses to the four guys, then exited the room.

"I'll work on getting you all specifically cleared to discuss everything but let me share with you just some thoughts." Jonathan painfully shifted his weight. "Please don't stand. I know there are at least four chairs in here. Guys, get a chair, and let's talk."

The men obliged, pushing up chairs next to the bed and settling into them.

Jonathan continued, "One of the challenges I'm now facing is trying to remain objective."

Frank's eyebrows lifted. "You? You're one of the most objective people I know."

"Frank, thanks for recognizing that. I pride myself on being steady, objective, even-keeled... Whatever ya wanna call it. But the more I learn, the more hate I feel for the president. She is cruel and vindictive and only serves herself. Her clandestine partnership with the Russians will destroy the United States." Jonathan looked away, absorbing the gravity of what he'd just said. "Everything she does is for her own benefit. She is the worst president this country has had, and I read this morning that her polling numbers are setting records! The American people have no clue." Eyes down, Jonathan shook his head.

Winston blew out a long breath. "I think maybe what's contributing to the way you feel is that it's all on you—you're doing it all on your own. After the Blake assassination, you had us, as I affectionally refer to it, as your sanity checkers. We would bounce ideas off one another—"

Brent interrupted, "And drink beers!"

The men all laughed.

"Yes, indeed," agreed Frank. "We also had scotch. Those were great but terrible times, but together, we survived and kept Brent from the electric chair!"

Jonathan looked wistful. "I wish I had a beer right now, but with these meds, I must wait a while. But being with you guys sure does bring my spirits up. So, let's put together some scenarios on how the next several weeks could go…?"

Chapter 14

Tuesday, November 10
US Capitol Complex, Washington, DC

It was 6:30 a.m. Sylvie was comfortably seated in the ornate reception area just outside of the chief architect's office. She had just finished reading the two Capitol Hill stalwart newspapers, *Roll Call* and *The Hill*, and was just starting *Politico* when Chief Architect Derek Monet walked in like a fresh breeze. Rather dapper in his gray fedora and black suit and his Burberry Westminster Heritage trench coat draped over his arm, he carried his briefcase with his free hand and looked up in surprise as he registered Sylvie's presence. With a big smile, he said, "Nice and early! Come into my office, and let's have coffee."

Sylvie stood, revealing an attractive, knee-length, violet-colored viscose dress with black-rivet, pointed-toe shoes.

Once the two of them were in his office, Derek turned and offered Sylvie a seat in an oversized leather chair. Sylvie sat and crossed her legs, smoothing the silky fabric over her knees, while Derek swiftly reached over and pressed the button on the Jura coffee machine, which immediately came to life.

Derek dropped his bag on his desk, tossed his overcoat on a nearby chair, then headed back to the machine, pressed another button, and the machine poured two coffees.

"How do you like yours?" he asked Sylvie.

"Black."

"Perfect. Me too." Derek handed Sylvie her coffee, then took the closest chair to her—also a large, oversized leather one.

Sylvie inhaled deeply, holding the cup under her dainty nose, then smiled. "This coffee smells divine."

"Oh, it's the best there is." He smiled, then added, "In this country, I mean. There's nothing like coffee on a sidewalk café in Paris."

Sylvie's smile broadened. "Parisian coffee is the only way I got through the Sorbonne!"

Derek's smile widened to match hers. "I can only imagine. I went to the University of Maryland, so it was pretty much Starbucks for me. Although, I did spend three months in Paris at the Sorbonne. I took classes and taught a class on architecture. Imagine that—an American teaching architecture in Paris! They treated me well, thank goodness."

Sylvie looked enchanted. "That's amazing. When were you there?"

"It was seven years ago. Might you have been there then?"

"Why, yes. I started at the Sorbonne at age seventeen and finished my studies after five years. While I can assure you, I did not take any architecture courses, imagine, we could have certainly been in the same hallways!"

Derek looked thoughtful. "Interesting, although I didn't just take architecture, but that would be a fun conversation at another time. I do have some good news. I've secured you an office in a quiet area in the Rayburn House Office Building. It's on the top floor with a nice window overlooking the Spirit of Justice Park. It should be ready for you to move in this morning. Oh, and if anyone were to ask, you are on special assignment to the speaker, and your term is indefinite."

Sylvie lowered her cup, eyes sparkling. "Oh, Mr. Monet… This is great news. Thank you so very much."

"You are most welcome, and please, call me Derek." His gaze became focused beyond Sylvie. He stood and moved to his desk, picking up the blinking phone. "Well, good morning, Madam speaker, we were just talking about you." After a slight pause, he added, "Who? Oh, your new resource from France, Sylvie Bardot." Another pause. "Yes, as a matter of fact, she will be in Dr. Bishop's old office on the fourth floor of the Rayburn." Derek paused again. "Yes, of course, I will let her know. Tell me, how are you doing?" Derek smiled after a few seconds. "That does not surprise me, and yes, of course, I will handle it…. Okay, I got it. Get well and talk to you later." Derek hung up and looked at Sylvie. "Wow, the speaker wants to be sure you are taken care of."

Sylvie cocked her head. "I'm flattered, but why me?"

Derek remained standing near his desk. "How well do you know the speaker?"

"Only what I've read, though I am looking forward to meeting her. Why? Is there something I should know?"

Derek, smiling, replied, "I think we'll discuss this maybe at the same time we talk about my Sorbonne curriculum. For now, I recommend you head over to the Longworth House Office Building cafeteria, where you can get a decent breakfast. It's the building right next to the Rayburn, where your office is." He gave a wave. "Head on over. I'll have someone meet you in fifteen or twenty minutes. They'll escort you up to your office and ensure you have everything you need."

Sylvie stood, placed her coffee cup and saucer on the table in front of her, and then turned toward the chief architect. "Thank you, Derek. It was very nice having coffee with you."

Derek's expression was warm, though his eyes revealed that he was distracted. "Won't be the last time. Please see yourself out. I have something that needs my attention right away."

Chapter 15

Tuesday, November 10
George Washington Hospital, Washington, DC

Jonathan awoke to the clinical touch of a nurse taking his vitals. Next to her stood Dr. Howard, looking on thoughtfully.

The doctor saw Jonathan's eyes open and smiled. "Good morning, Mr. Cartwright. Sorry to have woken you, but it is a good sign that you were sound asleep. How are you feeling?"

Jonathan reached for his water bottle and took a few swallows. "I slept like a rock. Other than stiffness and a slight headache, I have to admit I don't seem to be in as much pain."

"Excellent. We had you on an IV, but only for saline, no meds." Howard looked at the nurse. "Please remove the IV." Then, returning his gaze to Jonathan, he said, "I'm told your guests stayed for a couple of hours yesterday. That's too much. I need for you to have a quiet day today."

Jonathan frowned. "Dr. Howard, I'm sure it's nothing, but during the past few days, I've had brief moments where I suddenly couldn't remember the name of the person I was talking to. I wasn't even going to mention it to you, but then, twice yesterday, for not even thirty seconds, I was in a total state of confusion—I had trouble figuring out where I was."

Dr. Howard pulled a pen-sized light out of his white lab coat vest pocket and began examining Jonathan's eyes. While he continued to swing the device, flashing light from one pupil to the other, he said to the nurse, "Schedule an MRI, a CT, and a neurologic exam for Mr. Cartwright, STAT."

The nurse nodded and exited the room.

Dr. Howard, his voice calm, though his eyes seemed a bit more intense than before, said, "Mr. Cartwright, we'll get this checked out immediately."

The two men heard the sound of heels clacking on the floor and turned their heads, watching Tina enter the room.

Jonathan was the first to speak. "Good morning, beautiful." He flashed his most convincing smile. "Dr. Howard was just saying I'm doing great."

Before Tina could respond, Dr. Howard clarified, "I would say you're doing better, not necessarily great yet."

Tina glanced from the doctor to her husband. "Well, you do look more rested, and you have some nice color in your face."

Dr. Howard turned to Tina. "He's coming along. I would like to see him get plenty of rest, without so many visitors. You being the exception, of course." With one last glance at Jonathan, he added, "I need you to rest. I will be back late in the day to check on you."

Tina and Jonathan both thanked the doctor as he left the room.

Tina kissed Jonathan on the cheek.

Jonathan stared into his wife's beautiful eyes and felt some of the angst drain away—she always had that effect on him. "You're so wonderful to be here," he murmured. "I had a great meeting with the guy's last night. They stayed for almost three hours. Frank and Winston are coming back later today—I hope they don't run into Dr. Howard." He grinned.

Tina moved closer to Jonathan, her eyes pleading. "I really wish you would retire, the past several months have been such a drain on you and now it has become dangerous. Tina's eyes filled with tears. "They tried to kill you!"

Jonathan slowly shook his head. "Yes. I've been thinking more and more about retirement, but I can't possibly leave now. I'm so close to finishing this and you shouldn't worry, that was a freak incident, nothing like that will ever happen again."

Tina reached and held Jonathan's hand. "I was so scared and now I'm worried about you."

Jonathan's legs hurt, he struggled a bit to adjust his position, then tried to convince himself that he was OK, he forced a smile. "I'm fine, I'm feeling better and will be out of here soon."

Tina could see through his attempt. "You're not fine. You need time to recover, and I will do everything I can to help, but I do need you to think about what's next."

They held hands as they sat in silence. Jonathan thought to himself how lucky he was to have Tina. They had been together for twelve great years. Jonathan had two prior marriages which did not end well. He knew how lucky he was now and wished for more quality time with her, but he realized he was obsessed with finishing his work and exposing President Gentry for all her crimes and abuses of power.

Tina broke the silence and mentioned that she was going to head downstairs to get some coffee and would be right back so they could talk more. She stood and turned to leave just as the speaker was being wheeled in by an orderly.

"Good morning," Suzanne said brightly, gazing up at Tina. "You must be Mrs. Cartwright. I'm Suzanne Montgomery."

Tina smiled politely and offered a hand. "Madam Speaker, I am Tina. It's a pleasure and an honor to meet you."

"Oh, Tina, you needn't be so formal with me. Please call me Suzanne. I'm a huge fan of your husband, and I just need a few minutes to have a word with him."

"Well, I can share him with you," Tina offered. "He's a big fan of you too."

Suzanne smiled, and Tina thought she detected a blush.

Jonathan, with a big smile, asked the speaker, "How can I be of help?"

Tina waved before Suzanne could answer and headed out of the room. The speaker asked the orderly to move her closer to Jonathan's bed so that she could speak to him quietly. Once in position, she told the orderly to leave and please close the door—she would call him when needed.

As soon as the door clicked closed behind the orderly, Jonathan spoke. "You seem like you're doing quite well."

"Yeah, I'm fine. But I'm worried and didn't sleep at all last night," Suzanne admitted. "I have something I need to tell you, but I do not want you to react until you've heard the whole story."

Jonathan nodded. "Please."

"Jonathan, I believe there are sinister activities going on that I cannot explain, and other than my chief of staff, Jennifer Largent, no one knows."

Jonathan held his hand up. "Hold on one second." He grabbed his personal iPhone and texted Tina: *I'm sorry, but I may be talking with the speaker for a while.* He hit Send and then said to the speaker, "Just letting Tina know we may be a while."

Suzanne nodded.

Seconds later, Tina responded with: *No prob. There's a temporary art exhibit just a few blocks from here.*

Jonathan responded: *Go with security!!! XOX*

Tina's response: *Yes! XOX*

Jonathan put his phone down and gazed at Suzanne. "I'm all ears."

Suzanne took a breath. "A couple of days before that wacko wannabe assassin took a shot at me, I received this inner office envelope with a microSD card, blank address, and no note—just this little black plastic thing. I called Jennifer, my chief of staff, into my office because I had no idea what to do with it. Well, she plugged it into my computer, and up came your Blake assassination report—"

"*What?!*" interrupted Jonathan.

Suzanne waved impatiently. "Keep your voice down."

Jonathan tersely whispered, "What are you telling me?! You do understand, that is a highly classified, eyes-only artifact. What did you do with it?!"

"Jonathan, please calm down," Suzanne pleaded. "As the Speaker of the House, I, of course, have clearance, as does my chief of staff. So, Jennifer and I both read it."

Jonathan shook his head. "Oh my God! An eyes-only document that was to be read by the attorney general! You have violated numerous policies and laws!"

"Jonathan, relax. I'm not here to argue or critique your report. In fact, I thought it was superbly written. What I need is your help in figuring all this out. How and why did I, the Speaker of the House, receive this, and from whom?"

Jonathan took a deep breath, then winced at the pain in his shoulder. "Okay... This makes absolutely no sense." Jonathan thought for a moment, then realized, "The attorney general must be somehow compromised."

Suzanne's eyes widened. "Attorney general? Why?"

"I was the only one to have seen that report—because I wrote it," he said pointedly. "But last week, I emailed it through JWICS, our highest-level security mail server. It was addressed to the attorney general, no one else." Jonathan uncomfortably shifted his leg encased in the large cast. "I got an acknowledgement receipt, indicating he opened it. When he was in here last week, after I awoke from my accident, we had a conversation. So, of course, I asked what he thought of the report, and he just looked at me kind of funny and said he hadn't seen it!"

Suzanne's expression was dark. "Personally, you've got to wonder, Attorney General Edward Stanton was one of President Gentry's first appointments after President Blake was assassinated. I never liked or trusted him. I can share with you that there are some serious issues being investigated by both the minority and majority members of the Judiciary Committee. Personally, I have my hands full protecting myself from Elizabeth Gentry."

Jonathan pondered that. "Well, you've read the report. You know how damning it is for the president. So, let me ask you: Who do you believe would benefit the most from that report being lost?"

Suzanne's eyes glittered as if hatching a plan. "Well, Jonathan, I believe you and I can work together on this."

Jonathan lifted a hand as if to slow her train of thought. "How trustworthy is Jennifer Largent?"

"I trust her with my life."

Satisfied, Jonathan nodded. "Well, that'll have to do for now. I have some people I need for you to meet. I want Jennifer there as well. Let me work on the logistics. Obviously, since you and I are imprisoned in this place, we'll need to meet here."

Suzanne's shoulders, which had seemed a bit hunched, visibly lowered. "Thank you, Jonathan. I feel much better now that you know what I did."

Jonathan, however, did not look quite as pleased. "Uh-huh—and for the record, I'm not good with the fact that you read my report, but we have other things that we need to address now, and the first one is: Do not let Dr. Howard know that we met all morning. If he finds out, we'll both end up in solitary confinement!"

Suzanne winked.

The door to Jonathan's room opened, and the nurse, accompanied by a medical assistant with a wheelchair, walked in. "Mr. Cartwright, we're here to take you for some testing."

Chapter 16

Tuesday, November 10
The White House

President Elizabeth Gentry was enjoying her tabbouleh salad lunch as she sat alone in the private residence of the White House family dining room, where, in that very spot, just eight months earlier, former President John Blake collapsed and died. With a slight smile, she pondered how well everything had worked out. She had it made, her polling numbers were high, and her annoying, elderly husband was off in the Mideast, working on a peace deal that she knew would never happen. She was in control, her adoring population lapped up her every word, and her enemies were frightful. Best of all, the speaker and Jonathan Cartwright were both out of commission and no longer a threat. The world was perfect.

Nathan the butler came in to clear her dishes.

The president stood and began toward the West Sitting Hall. Without bothering to look at him, she ordered, "Nathan, I'll have coffee in here."

"Right away, ma'am."

President Gentry plopped down onto the sofa in the West Sitting Hall, kicked off her shoes, and put her feet up. Feeling for her phone, she found it eventually and called Wendy, her chief of staff. "Hey, Wendy, I don't feel like going back to the Oval this afternoon. I don't think there's anything major on my calendar. Actually, I don't care what's on it. Cancel it. Then I want you to come over so we can work. See you then." She disconnected the call, never allowing Wendy to say a word.

Gentry's burner cell phone buzzed; she looked down to read a text: *We have assets in position.*

Gentry responded: *Call me.*

Her burner phone rang, and she answered, "I want you to hold. Take no further action with your asset that is now working for the speaker. I believe we can use her relationship to our advantage."

Roman Mirov responded, "Yes, I see your point. What about Jonathan Cartwright?"

"With him being critically injured and in the hospital, he's no threat to us. I want you, for now, to just keep tabs on him and keep me informed. And you already assured me that his report will never see the light of day, so we're good."

"Perfect. Is there anything else we need to cover?"

"I need for you to keep tabs on all my cabinet members, especially the attorney general. I don't need any of them creating issues for us."

"Of course," Mirov answered, "and as you know, we already are tracking them, and I can provide you with a detailed report."

"Yes. Schedule it. I've got to go." Gentry clicked off her phone and put it on silent just as Wendy walked in.

"Hello, Madam President," greeted Wendy. "How are you?"

Wendy Wolf was a close personal acquaintance of Gentry's, having known the president since they went to Harvard together. Among her admirable credentials, Wendy had spent time as an intelligence analyst with the CIA and worked at the Securities and Exchange Commission. Forty-five years old and highly cerebral, she had remained a positively adorable blonde, built like a ballerina at five feet, five inches and 110 pounds. Add to that her sweet disposition, and she easily garnered a lot of attention from men but never really had the time to date. Elizabeth Gentry relied on Wendy to handle some of her more difficult and private tasks.

"Hey, Wendy," muttered Gentry. "I'm just feeling a little lazy today and like being relaxed up here where we can go over things."

Wendy smiled. "Perfect! I love it up here."

Gentry waved a hand. "So, what's important? What's next? You know the drill."

Wendy glanced at the iPad that seemed eternally glued to her hand. "We need to get you a vice president. It's been eight months. Interestingly, did you see the piece CNN ran last night? They suggested you may be proving that the role of vice president is meaningless."

Gentry grinned. "Yes, I watched it. I thought it was funny because they never mentioned the Constitution and the succession of power aspects. I'll pick someone soon, but I must admit, I'm having some fun dangling the role in front of some folks."

Wendy smirked. "You are too good at having fun!"

They both laughed.

"So, about the Chinese…?" Gentry's chief of staff inquired.

Gentry nodded. "Yes, I'm going to be the first president since Nixon to improve relations. There are many benefits to be realized by having the top two economies and military powers partner on some mutually beneficial things." Gentry reached over, pushing a button on the table near her. Within seconds, Nathan had walked through the door from the pantry. Gentry gazed at him placidly. "Please bring us glasses of cucumber water." Nathan nodded and left. Gentry continued, "I know that talk about the Chinese began with mentions of a possible state dinner."

"Yes, that's what you asked me to leak."

Gentry smiled. "Well done, my dear."

In quick time, Nathan reappeared with two tall, crystal glasses filled with cucumber slices swimming in clear water. He placed one on a coaster in front of the president and the other next to Wendy.

"Thank you, Nathan." Gentry then went on as if the butler was already gone. "Well, rather than a boring old state arrival, followed by meetings and then a state dinner, let's shake things up a bit. Let's host them somewhere special, and please, not Camp David. That's the oldest, moldiest, grungiest, Camp Granada-like place around."

Wendy smirked. "Great, now I'm gonna have that song in my head the rest of the day." Dramatically placing a hand on her chest, she intoned, "Hello, Mudduh. Hello, Fadduh. Here I am at…Camp Granada…!"

They laughed.

"I'm serious," Gentry cautioned. "It's the Chinese. Let's bring them someplace we can show off America. Give it some thought, then let's meet on it. Okay, what else do we have?"

Wendy glanced at her iPad. "The Speaker of the House has been in the hospital for several days now. You should probably offer a message of sympathy, flowers, or something."

Gentry looked very pleased. "The best thing for this country would be for that incompetent bitch to rot to death in that hospital!"

Wendy trying her best to conceal her smile. "Hmmm, okay. So, maybe just flowers?"

Gentry paused for a second. "I admit, I went a tad overboard, so maybe not *rot in hell*. Here's hoping she falls out of the twelfth-floor window. Um, so, yeah, send flowers."

"Shall we discuss the budget?"

Gentry snorted. "Nope. Let's review my upcoming trips."

"Next week, you're going to Baltimore to dedicate the new hospital ship."

The president's expression soured. "Okay, let me rephrase that. What fun trips are coming up?!"

"Five days: West Coast, San Francisco, for a technology conference, followed by the Sonoma Wine Conference."

Gentry leaned back. "Now, that's what I'm talking about!"

"Well, with less than twelve months until the election, there are a lot of day trips coming up that we're finding will match well with your political agenda."

Gentry rolled her eyes. "Yeah, yeah, yeah. I know. Fill up my calendar with those, but spice 'em up a bit. What I mean is, say I'm in Salt Lake talking about solar energy and expanding the national parks. But while I'm there, get me at least six hours on the slopes at Park City!"

Wendy was about to speak when her cell phone rang. She answered, paused for a few seconds, then said, "Yes, she's here. We're meeting together." Another pause. "What?!" Wendy turned to the president with a serious look. "This happened just now?" After a longer pause this time, Wendy said, "Got it. Goodbye."

Wendy put down her phone and announced to Gentry, "Thirty minutes ago, a Russian missile overshot Ukraine and landed in Moldova. Casualties reported."

The president stood. "Shit. Let's get everybody in the Situation Room."

Both women had started toward the elevator when the president stopped abruptly. "Go ahead without me," Gentry directed. "I'll be right there. I need to call Vladimir."

. . .

Not too long afterward, President Gentry called her chief of staff. Wendy answered.

"Wendy," Gentry began over the line, "no need for us to meet in the Situation Room. I just talked to President Putin. He assured me there was no Russian missile that entered Moldova. I need you to, first of all, ensure that no word reaches the press that I talked to Putin. Second of all, ask the secretary of defense to report to me on how we could misidentify a missile entering Moldova. That will be all."

The phone went dead.

Chapter 17

Tuesday, November 10
Capitol Hill, Washington, DC

Sylvie answered her desk phone. "Sylvie Bardot."

"Jennifer Largent!" Jennifer announced. "So sorry I haven't gotten up to see you yet. I've been in meetings all day. How are you doing?"

Sylvie glanced toward the broad pane of glass in her side wall. "You mean other than staring out my window at this magnificent view?"

"Ha!" laughed Jennifer. "You know what I hate? Phones. I'm coming over to see you now. Be there in a minute." Jennifer hung up.

Sylvie returned the phone to its cradle, then swiveled her chair back to her computer and resumed typing.

Ten minutes later, Jennifer came in through the door. Sylvie turned her chair to fully face her as Jennifer offered a bottle of water.

"Here you go. It's very easy to dehydrate in these old buildings."

Sylvie opened the bottle. "Perfect. I've been up here for a while and lost total track of time." She took a drink, then reached to the printer at the edge of her credenza, lifted a stack of paper from it, and handed it to Jennifer. "Here you go. It's pretty rough, but I'd like to get your thoughts on whether you believe this may be of help."

Jennifer looked at the title: "Emerging Trade Agreements of Europe." She felt the weight of the document, her eyes meeting Sylvie's. "What the hell? This must be fifty pages. Did you create this from ChatGPT?!" She shook her head as she flipped through the pages in a rush.

Sylvie laughed. "Heck, no! Oh, and it's sixty-seven pages. I started it last night. Of course, this is just me taking a shot in the dark on what it is the speaker might like. The document is a summary of the current trends.

It primarily focuses on the EU, but I did include some pages specific to Russia."

Jennifer flopped into a seat, still browsing the document. "I cannot believe this. I can tell just from reading a few paragraphs that the speaker will love it."

Sylvie smiled. "If you believe I'm on the right track, give me another day to make it better."

"Great! I'm very pleased. Good work. Hey, you've done enough for today, and with the speaker still in the hospital, I'm not chained here until 10 p.m. like usual. How about you and I head over to Bullfeathers and grab a drink?!"

Sylvie's smile was as pleasant as ever. "Sounds great. I'd love to."

. . .

Jennifer led Sylvie into the loud and crowded bar. It was predominantly filled with Hill staffers and a few political consultants and lobbyists. As the two women made their way to the actual bar to order drinks, Jennifer nodded and smiled at the happy-hour participants. Two stools suddenly became vacant. As Jennifer and Sylvie took their seats, Jennifer turned to thank the two junior staffers who had given them up. The junior staff always leaped at any opportunity to do something for the speaker's chief of staff.

Jennifer, raising her voice so she could be heard, asked Sylvie what she would like.

Sylvie glanced around the room, then smiled. "I think I'm interested in trying some local IPAs."

Jennifer smiled. "Perfect. Me too! Would you like for me to order for you?"

Sylvie reading the board above the bar pondered, then decided, "I think I would like to try a Capit-ale IPA."

Jennifer looked surprised, then laughed and yelled, "Great!" She got the bartender's attention. "I'd like a bottle of Dogfish Head 60 Minute, and she'll have a draft Capit-ale."

Jennifer scooted her bar stool closer to Sylvie. "There, now I don't have to yell."

Sylvie nodded. "Yes, it's quite loud and very crowded in here."

Jennifer smirked. "You know, the speaker and I have come in here a few times. You should see the reaction we get."

Sylvie smiled back with a raised eyebrow. "Does it get really quiet?"

"No, just the opposite. People adore the speaker. She's a lot of fun, and in any bar on Capitol Hill, everyone goes crazy when she walks in. We have a blast!"

The bartender placed their drinks on the bar, and Jennifer handed him a twenty, telling him that he could keep the change. The bartender smiled and offered, "Jennifer, you're always so good to us. Thanks!"

Sylvie leaned toward Jennifer. "The bartender knows your name?"

Jennifer burst out laughing. "Honey, all the bartenders in this town know my name!"

They both sat for a while, just drinking their beers and people-watching.

Sylvie leaned toward Jennifer. "Are you married?"

Jennifer, in a soft voice, responded, "No, I was engaged a couple of times, but work is pretty much my partner in life." She took a drink from her bottle. "How about you? Any handsome French men in your life?"

Sylvie, with a smile, said, "I can honestly say, no." Her smile faded as she continued, "Actually, I'm still reeling from a pretty difficult end to a relationship from earlier this year— but I can't get into that."

Jennifer thought for a moment, and decided not to pry, "Well, I'm always here if you want to talk about it. Or together we can drink our sorrows away!"

Sylvie let out a quick laugh, "So, tell me, how is the speaker's recovery going?"

"I had breakfast with her this morning at 6:30, and thankfully, since she's the speaker, the food wasn't too bad. But overall, I think she's doing well. She's got all her energy, that's for sure. But she probably won't be back for at least another ten days or so."

Sylvie gazed at her over her glass. "So, you've been working for the speaker for over ten years?"

"Twelve! I worked for her before she became speaker. I can't believe the time has gone by so fast." She shook her head, eyes going cloudy with nostalgia.

"It must be demanding work. Is she okay to work with?"

Jennifer's gaze brightened again. "I love her, really. She is the absolute best boss I've ever had. She treats me well and always has my back. Heck, I work eleven-plus hours a day because I believe in her, and I want her to succeed. You've only seen the bravado side of her, when she gives a tough speech or is fending off an attack on the floor of the House. But in private, she's kind, considerate, and has a great sense of humor. We work hard, and we play hard."

Sylvie quietly digested that. "Thanks for sharing this. It really is helpful."

Jennifer glanced around, then leaned in again. "I should share something else with you. Years ago, before she became a congresswoman, she lost her husband and daughter in a plane crash."

Sylvie's mouth opened. "Oh my God, what a terrible thing. Did she have any other children?"

Jennifer shook her head sadly. "No, and she never remarried."

Sylvie looked away. "That's so sad. I cannot imagine."

"She has never stopped thinking about it," Jennifer divulged. "I believe she suffers a great deal."

"Wow," Sylvie breathed. "She's done incredibly well despite what must have been a horrible ordeal."

"You'll end up loving her, you'll see," assured Jennifer, taking a swig from her bottle.

Sylvie smiled. "So, tell me about Derek Monet, does he have a wife and children?"

Jennifer answered, "No wife, no children. Derek is gay."

Sylvie leaned back, surprised. "Oh, I had no idea!"

Jennifer, after clearly holding back a chuckle, continued, "He's a bit old-school. He keeps his private life very private. Hardly anyone knows."

Sylvie nodded. "He seems like a good person."

"He's an incredibly good person, very honest and extremely trustworthy. He is the epitome of class, tact, and diplomacy. We—the speaker and I—love him to death!"

A man slowly emerged from the crowd and stood near Jennifer until she finally looked up at him. "Oh, hi, Popov. Haven't seen you for over a week. How's life in the world of lobbying?"

Popov, a big and tall man who wore expensive suits and, judging by his five o'clock shadow, looked like he had to shave twice a day, reached between the two ladies to place his scotch on the bar, ensuring they got an up close and personal view of his gold Rolex and his ruby cufflinks—which alone probably cost more than Jennifer's car.

Popov then straightened and said to Jennifer while unabashedly leering at Sylvie, "Are you going to introduce us?"

Jennifer, concealing her exasperation, obliged. "Popov, this is Sylvie. She just started working for the speaker."

Popov shook Sylvie's hand…and would not let go. "Oh, lovely." He flashed pearl-white teeth. "Welcome aboard. I see the speaker all the time. I hope we have an opportunity to work together." He finally released his sweaty grasp on her fingers.

Sylvie just nodded, retracting her hand without saying a word.

Popov turned to Jennifer. "I sent the speaker flowers. I tried to go see her, but the nurses said she was not accepting visitors. Makes sense. Anyway, please let her know I was asking about her and am looking forward to seeing her soon."

"Of course, Popov. I'll pass along the message—and good seeing you." Jennifer turned away and faced another greeter, a man from the Ways and Means Committee.

Popov looked back at Sylvie, thrilled at seeing that she had no male companion with her. He stepped closer to her and leaned down.

Sylvie was immediately overcome by his strong cologne. *God, this is awful*, she thought. *Who wears cologne these days?*

Popov purred, "If there is ever anything you need, please don't hesitate to ask." He then handed her his card and continued, "I've been around this town a long time, and there are very few that I don't know. I'm sure I can help you." He stood, nodded, and then walked away. Sylvie, having uttered not a word during the entire exchange, was happy to see him go.

Jennifer said goodbye to her greeter, then turned back toward Sylvie, asking if she wanted another beer.

"No, thank you. I've had a long day." She drained the remaining amber liquid from her glass and set it down on the glossy counter. "I think I'm gonna head back to my place."

"Good. Me too." She set her bottle down with a *thunk*. "Let's get out of here."

The two women exited onto First Street, then made a right on D. It was a pleasant autumn night. The streetlights cast a soft glow on the sidewalk. The only sounds were an occasional car driving by and the clicking of their high heels on the concrete walk.

Jennifer looked ahead. "Your place is on 4th Street?" After Sylvie's nod, Jennifer added, "I live off East Capitol so I can walk with you part of the way."

Sylvie frowned. "That guy, Popov... He was creepy."

Jennifer shook her head, walking with Sylvie down the street. "Yeah, rich and creepy. He pretends to be a lobbyist. I don't know that he actually does anything except donate a lot of money to various candidates. His parents are both dead. His father was rumored to be a Russian oligarch and allegedly left him a lot of money."

As they walked along D Street, Sylvie nonchalantly pulled Popov's business card and stared at it, committing the name and contact info to memory. Popov. Karl Popov.

Chapter 18

Tuesday, November 10
4th Street SE, Capitol Hill, Washington, DC

Sylvie entered her apartment, locked the door, threw her bag on a nearby chair, and then sat on her sofa and turned on the Sangean FM radio, which was tuned to WETA classical. She removed her shoes and began to relax, feeling content as she reminisced over her recent days in Washington. She was actually enjoying her role as Sylvie Bardot, a cool, smart, attractive, and young Hill staffer. She thought about all the young men who had smiled at her as she walked past them in Bullfeathers. In her prior life as Annika Antonov, she had never received that sort of attention from men.

Her life as Annika was still painfully fresh in her mind—where she still often relived the relationship she had developed during her last assignment in the US. It had ended tragically. She had found her true soulmate, something that Annika knew she would never be able to get past. She could not stop wondering what their lives together would have been like and found herself constantly battling feelings of emptiness, sorrow, and tremendous guilt for reasons she wasn't yet able to fully comprehend.

But her time with Jennifer Largent had brightened her spirits. Jennifer seemed so nice, supportive, and encouraging; she could turn out to be a good friend. Sylvie was looking forward to meeting the speaker, and from what she had learned thus far, she knew she would like her.

She glanced at her Apple Watch: 7:30. No wonder she was hungry. After entering her tiny kitchen and pulling out a single-serving yogurt cup from her fridge, her cell phone buzzed. She checked the screen, noting a text message from Roman Mirov. It read: *Meet me at Russia House*.

Damn, she thought, *I was looking forward to a quiet and early night.* She responded to the text with: *ETA 20 minutes*.

She quickly finished her yogurt and changed into something more appropriate.

. . .

The Russia House, Northwest DC

The Russia House Restaurant, an aging establishment perched at the corner of Florida and Connecticut avenues NW, had been the go-to place for Russians in DC for years and remained so. The eatery had consistently earned decent reviews, and, it being fall, was still mild enough for patrons to enjoy the outdoor seating.

Sylvie, garbed in black jeans, a black leather jacket, and a black Polo ballcap, trotted up the entry steps, ignoring the outside dining guests. She walked in and headed directly to the bar, selecting a seat at the far end where she and Roman Mirov could be alone. A minute hadn't passed before the bartender placed two Mamont vodkas in front of her, then discreetly walked to the other end of the bar.

Sylvie wasn't particularly in the mood for vodka, but never one to dishonor the Yukagir Mammoth, she picked up the closest glass out of the pair and took a sip. As she was setting it down again, Roman suddenly appeared on her right. He put his arm around her shoulder, giving her a squeeze.

Sylvie smiled. "Roman, good to see you."

Roman's eyes swept over her. "I like that all-black stealthy look." He returned her smile, then grabbed his glass and took a drink. Pulling his bar stool as close as possible to Sylvie without being on top of her, he took another pull of his drink, then swallowed, licked his lips, and stared at her with his hard eyes. "How are you settling in? Do you need anything?"

"All's well. I love the apartment and am enjoying the work."

"Good, just don't like it too much." He flashed a toothy grin and took another big swallow of his vodka. "Tell me, how close will you be able to get to the speaker?"

Sylvie had her answer ready: "I believe, once she's back from the hospital, I will have a chance to meet her."

Roman's dark eyes lit up. "Excellent. Our assignment has been slightly altered. We are not to eliminate the speaker. For now, we are to get as close as we can to her, then stand by for further instructions."

Sylvie nodded. "Got it, no elimination at this point. What about Jonathan Cartwright?"

"As long as he's hospitalized, he will not be a priority. However, should somehow the opportunity present itself, I will rely on you to use your best judgment and handle it." Roman looked to his right, got the bartender's attention, and ordered them more drinks. He then continued, "I need you to read the assassination report." Roman handed her a tiny microSD card. "Read it tonight, then destroy it."

The bartender placed the drinks on the bar, though Sylvie wasn't even halfway through her first one. Roman noticed and commented, "Are you okay?" He then gulped down a significant amount of the vodka poured into his new glass.

Sylvie straightened. "Oh, I'm fine. I probably should head out, get this report read, then get some sleep."

Roman mock-toasted her.

As Sylvie got off her barstool, she reached into her jacket, then handed Roman Karl Popov's card. "Do me a favor. Please have this guy checked out. Thanks."

Roman slipped the card into his blazer pocket.

As Sylvie walked away, she turned back and waved to a grinning Roman, who was now holding his glass as well as hers.

Chapter 19

Wednesday, November 11
Washington, DC

The door to Sylvie's office swung wide open, and in walked Jennifer. "Good morning! We're going on a field trip!" Jennifer put a large to-go coffee cup on Sylvie's desk. "C'mon, grab your coffee. Let's go. I'm serious."

Sylvie, a bit bewildered and amused, could only mutter, "What?"

"The speaker wants to meet you. The car is waiting for us on Independence Avenue." She jerked a thumb toward the door behind her. "Let's move it!"

Sylvie grabbed her coffee and her jacket, and the two dashed out.

. . .

Jennifer pressed the button for the sixth floor, and the elevator began to move.

Sylvie was surprised at her slightly nervous anticipation; she never had felt nervous about much of anything before.

They stepped off the elevator. Sylvie remained several feet behind Jennifer, watching her companion enter the nurse's station. After a few seconds, she heard the lady at the station say, "Yes, she's expecting you. Go to room 611, straight down the hallway. Make a left. It's the fourth room on the right."

Jennifer nodded and glanced back at Sylvie, waiting for her to catch up. The pair then walked the long hallway. As soon as they made the left at the corner, two well-armed commandos in black with bright-white FBI lettering stopped them and asked for their IDs. After providing the requested credentials, the women were allowed to continue.

The entry to room 611 was guarded by another uniformed FBI agent, who acknowledged them and opened the door. As they walked in, the agent mentioned, "She's down the hall."

Jennifer and Sylvie stood in the hospital room for a moment, admiring its surprising size. Even the window seemed extra-large.

A nurse came in; Jennifer recognized her from the last time she was there. The woman stood before the two women and said in a no-nonsense tone, "The speaker asked that you all come with me."

The trio of women exited the room, made a sharp right, then continued past a few rooms until they got to 618, where another FBI agent stood and waved them in.

The nurse who had escorted them stood off to the side, and Jennifer followed by Sylvie entered the room.

Less than ten feet in front of her sat the speaker, her leg fully extended from her wheelchair in a bright white cast. Beyond the speaker, seated upright in bed, sat a tall man wearing a sling. He, too, sported a full-length white cast, supported by a half-dozen pillows. Sylvie suddenly felt a sinking feeling in the pit of her stomach as she realized she was staring at the man who, only eight months ago, shot and left her for dead during a blizzard in the back streets near the White House.

"Sylvie... Sylvie?"

Sylvie snapped to attention.

The speaker went on, "We're very pleased to have someone with your fine credentials, and I can tell you, it's official. You are now on permanent loan from the French government."

Sylvie blinked and, realizing she must look like a mental patient, forced herself to focus and her lips to move. "Why, thank you, Madam Speaker. It's an honor to meet you, and I am so grateful for your arranging for me to be here."

The speaker turned toward Jonathan. "Sylvie, in just one day with us, has written an outstanding summary for me on European Trade." The speaker paused. "Oh, pardon. Sylvie Bardot, meet Jonathan Cartwright, the director of the Office of Intelligence for the National Security Division."

Sylvie's feet felt cemented to the ground. Finally, she forced her head to nod and gave a slight smile.

Jonathan smiled. "Sylvie, welcome. It sounds like we're very fortunate to have you on board. I must apologize. I was not expecting guests. Please pardon my current state—I look forward to properly meeting you when I'm out of here."

The speaker waved a hand, eager to move forward. "Okay, Jonathan, thank you for your time. We will continue our discussion later."

The nurse then moved behind the speaker's wheelchair and propelled it out of the room. Sylvie and Jennifer left next, closing the door quietly behind them.

Once in the hallway, the speaker's apparently calm front disintegrated. She glared daggers at Jennifer and snarled, "I did not want anyone in that room! That was a complete embarrassment to me and the director." She bared her white teeth. "Jesus Christ, *what were you thinking?!*"

Jennifer, ever-calm, quietly answered, "Let's talk about this when we get back to your room."

They entered the room, where the speaker, still angry, grumbled, "What a ridiculous situation you've put me in."

The nurse, still clutching the handles of the wheelchair, took in a shuddering breath. "Mrs. Speaker." Her cry quickly devolved into a sob.

Jennifer, always ready for anything, immediately reached into her handbag and handed the distraught woman a tissue.

"Oh, thank you, honey." The nurse blew her nose and continued, "Ms. Speaker, I found your staff in here and told them to follow me."

The speaker, now a bit calmer, said, "I had asked for you to bring my chief of staff, not all my staff." The speaker then laughed. "It's okay." She looked toward Sylvie. "My apologies. I don't typically get upset with things. I hope you were not embarrassed by being escorted into some random man's hospital room."

Sylvie, still bewildered by the exchange she'd just witnessed, said in a near whisper, "No. Everything is fine."

Suzanne now met her gaze solidly. "Sylvie, I wanted to spend some time with you to share just how impressed I was with your report, and how pleased I am that you'll be able to work for us officially." Her gaze slid over to Jennifer. "Jenny, darling, please forgive me for my outburst. Whew, that was crazy." She rolled her eyes playfully. "When's the last time I did that?!"

Jennifer shrugged. "I dunnoh... Yesterday?"

Everyone in the room laughed, and with the mood settling, the women got down to business.

Chapter 20

Wednesday, November 11
Michael's Drive, Bethesda, MD

Delun Li, a tall, athletic man in his thirties, read quietly while he sat at the kitchen table. In the other room, he heard tiles clicking as the men launched into their third hour of Mahjong.

The house on Michael's drive in Bethesda, typical of what one would find in the upper-class suburbs of Washington, DC, was as quiet and private as any other on that street. The yard was suitably lovely, the kitchen was spacious, and all the other rooms were large and well-furnished. The man who owned the house was overseas working for the State Department—he'd been assigned to the Ethiopian embassy in Addis Ababa and thus had no problem renting the house to Delun Li, a government technology consultant.

Delun looked at the clock on the microwave: 3:10. From the dining room, he heard one of the men shout: 'mahjong!' followed by clapping. Delun, who had been awaiting such an outcry from one of the men, called, "Gentlemen, I've just poured us some Johnnie Walker Double Black, neat. Please join me in the kitchen so we can get started."

The four older men sauntered into the kitchen, found their glasses, and seated themselves around the large table.

Delun began by holding up his glass. "Gentlemen, I would like to propose a toast." He met the eyes of the oldest man among them. "Professor, I think you will be pleased by my research." His eyes then moved among the rest of the kitchen occupants. "You all have been brought here to assist with a very important assignment. As you know, I am the representative to the Ministry of State Security. I have been appointed by the Standing Committee of the National People's Congress. My classification and assignments are of a critical nature all for the success of our People's Republic." He then intoned, "Let's stand."

All the men rose to their feet. Delun drank; the men followed. Delun sat down, and again, the men followed his example.

Delun spoke on. "Gentlemen, while you were playing games in the other room, I was reading a remarkable document: the Department of Justice's report on the assassination of President Blake. We caught a break. The company I work for in the United States has an information technology support contract with the Department of Justice, and thanks to my due diligence, I was successful in obtaining this artifact, which will advance our cause."

Delun picked up the report, stood, and slowly walked around the table. "Not only does this report expose the current president's many crimes, but it also provides an alarming picture of how the Russians have been able to manipulate the White House! In fact, in addition to this report, we have learned, through other sources, that the Russians are still heavily involved in controlling President Elizabeth Gentry!"

Delun paused for effect by his empty chair, then peered into each man's eyes as if gauging his worth. "I want you to know, the chairman has asked me to come up with a plan to replace the Russians!" Delun slammed the report on the table, then continued, "I am to report my progress directly to the chairman and his senior advisors." Delun then walked back to the head of the table and took his seat. "Gentlemen, for the next several hours, I will be sharing with you ideas regarding how we can accomplish the chairman's request." Delun took a sip from his drink, then smiled. The men all returned his expression, eager to hear their boss's thoughts.

Chapter 21

Thursday, November 12
George Washington Hospital, Washington, DC

The television, suspended from the ceiling seven feet above the foot of Jonathan's bed, was turned to CNN. News anchors were reporting on the surprise presidential veto of the jobs bill.

Jonathan squinted into the early morning sun as he leaned close to the window, struggling to close the curtain. A wave of dizziness nearly overcame him, and it was an effort to focus. Feeling a slight sense of accomplishment as he managed to finish his task, he then sat back and continued to watch TV without the glare of sunlight bothering him.

"President Blake had been very involved in the jobs bill. In fact, CNN was told the former president helped write it. The veto came as a shock to the Senate, which had passed it overwhelmingly. The bill's sponsor, Senator Ron Young of Pennsylvania, was distraught as he talked to reporters."

The screen switched to footage of Young, who said with remorse into the camera, "This is a sad day. This bill would have been one more accomplishment to add to the legacy of our wonderful former president."

The report was interrupted by CNN Breaking News. The previous anchor who'd spoken before the Young footage reported, "CNN has just learned that President Gentry is going to select Georgia Governor Celine Johnson to be her nominee for vice president. Johnson is seventy-three years old and has been the governor of Georgia for the past five years. She would be only the second African American vice president."

Jonathan, with an eye roll, grabbed the remote after digging it out from beneath his sheets and turned off the TV. He picked up his cold coffee, about to take an unpleasant sip, when he heard a knock at his door. *No one bothers knocking*, he thought with a raised eyebrow—then looked up to see the door open and Bartholomew Winston enter, carrying two coffee cups.

Jonathan, his worries temporarily erased, smiled broadly. "Winston! So nice to see you. Pull up a chair."

Winston glanced at the cup still in Jonathan's hand. "Sorry to see you already have coffee."

Jonathan tossed his cup into the nearby trashcan in relief. "I'm absolutely sure what you brought is better than what they have here!"

Winston obligingly handed Jonathan a cup. "This is from Peet's—always consistent in my book."

Jonathan took a sip of the rich, full-bodied brew. "Wow, this is wonderful, thanks." Jonathan adjusted the pillow under his cast, then said, "Hey, I'm having some difficulties arranging the logistics for our group meeting here at the hospital. It probably would be best to do it after I'm discharged, hopefully in ten days. Will you still be around?"

"For you? Absolutely." Smiling, Winston added, "In between, I may spend a few days up in Philadelphia."

"Good." Jonathan closed his eyes and took another body-warming sip. "By the way, how's that going?"

Winston seemed pleased at the question. "The former first lady, Beverly, is a good soul. We very much enjoy our time together, have traveled to Europe twice, and have also gone to many of the national parks in the west. As I mentioned, Antarctica may be next."

Jonathan smiled warmly. "I'm so happy for you, Winston. How's San Diego? How are Win and Gail and the twins?"

"Amazing! My condo is not far from them. We have dinner together several times a week. I love going over for breakfast before they go to work. My job is making silly faces at the twins while they eat. They have a wonderful nanny who comes each weekday. I just hang around for thirty minutes or so to help the nanny for a bit, although she's darn good and doesn't need me. I think she lets me hang around a little just to feel needed! Ha!"

Jonathan absorbed all that lighthearted talk of young kids at breakfast time as if hearing the inside details of some sacred ritual. "I missed all that in life… Tina nor I ever had children." Jonathan, careful to keep the sadness from his expression, sipped more coffee.

Winston realized he needed to change the subject, "Hey, by the way, I visited Loretta Fitzgerald at Saint Elizabeth's Psychiatric Hospital a few months ago."

Jonathan, looking surprised, "Wow, how did she seem?"

"She was pleased to see me, but I can tell she's lonely and way too thin. She spends every waking moment with her head in a book, which she told me distracts her from reality." Winston said somberly.

Jonathan looked down, "It's so sad how things turned out for her being committed; Loretta spent two dozen years in the White House as an assistant usher to you. No one could have predicted that she would have been the only person charged in the assassination of President John Blake."

There was a knock at the door, Jonathan looked up and saw his employee—his best technical resource, his go-to guy for any and all variety of emergencies—enter the room. Suddenly, Jonathan froze in horror. He couldn't remember his employee's name. Anxiety filled him as he realized he had to say something. His pulse rose, and he felt hot, helplessness, and desperation fusing into anger. *What's wrong with me?! I hired this guy!* Just as sweat began to emerge on his forehead, the name bolted back into his brain. *Tim!* After what seemed like an awkward pause, he grinned and waved him over. "Hey, Tim. Good to see you. Come on in." He looked at Winston. "Winston, I need just a few minutes…" Another uncomfortable pause ensued as Jonathan temporarily lost his employee's name a second time. "…with Tim," he finally managed. "Do you mind?"

Winston jumped up. "I need to get a walk in. I'll check back in an hour or so." He left the room.

"Perfect," Jonathan said after him, then met Tim's gaze. "Come on over. What have we learned?"

Tim did as asked, taking Winston's vacated chair. "Okay, first things first: regarding the attorney general saying he never got your assassination report email… I met with the JWICS systems administrator and his boss. As you can imagine, they are taking this incident very seriously. They are able to track your email from the time it left Mount Weather all the way to the AG's JWICS connection in his office. There were no errors or interruptions in the transmission. Everything looks good. JWICS is having their three top-tier techs at DOJ inspect the AG's computer to see if they can find any problems."

Jonathan frowned thoughtfully. "This is so weird. I need to see it from my workstation and make sure the file is still accessible."

Tim nodded. "We can check that too."

"Good. Please do."

Tim opened his laptop and moved closer so that Jonathan could see. Tim glanced around the room, then said in a low voice, "Okay... I'm not sure what we're allowed to talk about in here."

Jonathan waved him on. "Go ahead. This is a matter of National Security. I authorize you to share with me classified information in this location." Jonathan then couldn't help but think, *Oh, jeez, I'm violating, like, eleven Intelligence Community directives right now!*

Tim took a breath, then tapped a few commands on his keyboard. "You directed us to monitor Russia House," he said, face lit by his monitor's screen. "And whenever Roman Mirov appeared, we were to store all our surveillance photos. Well, he was there on November 10, from 17:07 until 23:51." Tim brought up a screen, which displayed four quadrants—in each quadrant was a photo's image. "Here are photos of each of the eighty-seven people that entered and exited during those approximate six and a half hours."

Jonathan smiled in approval. "This is great." At his request, Tim slowly moved from one screen to the next. After several minutes spent studying forty-four screens of photos, and just when he was about to stop, Jonathan blurted out, "Hey! Wait a minute." Jonathan studied the photo of a woman for several seconds, then shook his head and sighed. "Never mind. I'm done."

Chapter 22

Friday, November 13
George Washington Hospital, Washington, DC

It was just after 7 a.m. Jonathan sat in bed staring at the TV, which was muted. He ignored the captioned text, choosing instead to gaze out the window at the falling rain. He still had not shared his recent memory lapses with Tina. The last thing she needed was something else to worry about, but he was concerned, even scared. Why was his brain doing this? His deep thoughts were interrupted when Dr. Howard entered his room.

Jonathan gave him a nod. "Good morning, Doc."

"Jonathan, how are you this morning?"

Jonathan exhaled slowly. "You tell me."

Dr. Howard glanced at the iPad he held in both hands. "I would like to discuss your neurological exam. I've had the results since Wednesday afternoon but wanted to wait until I had the opinions of another doctor." His eyes flickered from the iPad to Jonathan. "Before we start, I need for you to understand, everything at this point is preliminary. We will likely need to perform additional tests."

Jonathan bit his bottom lip. "Dr. Howard, Tina does not know anything about this."

Dr. Howard frowned. "You need to share this with her."

"Oh, I will, but not yet. I just don't want to add any further burden on her, so please, if she walks in, stop the conversation."

Dr. Howard's brow furrowed. "I'll do as you request, but I don't agree with it."

"Thanks. So, spill it. What do we know?"

"Let's start by confirming some of the information we got from you when you first woke up here in the hospital," the doctor began. "Just some basic questions. Do you drink?"

Jonathan flashed a devilish smile. "Not enough!" After sharing a brief laugh with the doctor, Jonathan continued, "I will have a glass of red wine with dinner—typically four or five nights per week. I enjoy an occasional beer, and on rare occasions, like, maybe once every couple of months, I'll have a sip of bourbon, sometimes scotch. My only true addiction is caffeine. I'll have one very strong cup of coffee in the morning, then that's it."

Dr. Howard took notes as Jonathan spoke. "Okay." He stopped tapping on the screen. "As I said, we got your medical history when you came in, but let's go over some of it again. Share with me the highlights, starting with your parents' health."

"I've been lucky, healthy my entire life. Never any meds, except until recently. My dad was healthy his entire life. He died at age ninety of COVID. My mom died years earlier at age eighty-six from Alzheimer's."

"In your lifetime, have you ever experienced any memory or cognitive issues?" asked Dr. Howard.

Jonathan shifted his weight in the bed. "None, until now. And having a mother that died of Alzheimer's.

You can understand why my recent experiences scare the hell out of me."

Dr. Howard lowered his iPad. "Since the other day when you shared with me times that you've forgotten the name of the person you were talking to, and your mention that you had experienced a significant state of confusion at one point, not knowing where you were, have there been any other occurrences?"

Jonathan glanced away. "Just the name thing. It happened a couple of times, and thankfully, the 'feeling lost' episodes have not reoccurred."

Dr. Howard, referring to his iPad, remarked, "I see you'll be sixty-eight in January."

"Yep, January 8."

"The results of your MRI and CT indicate that everything is normal," reported Dr. Howard. "And the EEG did not show any indication of seizure. I'm having the results reviewed, but initially, it looks good."

Jonathan released the breath he hadn't realized he'd been holding. "Well, that's good news, right?"

"Yes, of course. The EEG results contain a tremendous amount of data, and it just takes longer to finalize, but so far, so good."

Dr. Howard started to leave, then stopped and turned to face Jonathan. "By the way, earlier, when I asked you about meds, you responded that you had never been on meds until recently. I assumed you were referring to meds from your accident, but were you ever on any other meds prior to the accident?"

Jonathan frowned. "Oh, sorry I wasn't clear. For the past two months, I've been on Metformin to lower my glucose numbers. But the last time I took it was the day of my accident. So, eleven days ago."

Dr. Howard pursed his lips. "Have you experienced any of the known side effects since you started the Metformin?"

Jonathan rolled his shoulders, thinking. "Well, yeah, just about every one of them that I've mentioned: hearing loss, ringing ears, headaches, stomach pain, loss of energy, memory loss and confusion, and constipation."

"Okay. For now, please hold off on taking Metformin. As for long-term, consult with your primary care physician."

Chapter 23

Saturday, November 14
George Washington Hospital, Washington, DC

Frank and Winston entered Jonathan's room, Frank carrying a cardboard cupholder that held three large coffees balanced in one hand and his briefcase in the other.

Frank handed one of the cups to Jonathan. "Good morning. It's a bright and cold November morning out there. How are you doing?"

Frank and Winston pulled two chairs over to be closer to Jonathan's bed.

"I'm doing okay," Jonathan reported. "Had some scares yesterday." Jonathan summarized his memory issues, leaving out no detail.

Winston and Frank exchanged a glance. "Have they shared the results from your tests?"

"Yes. Some of the tests, all looked OK, and they'll be doing more tests soon." Jonathan idly glanced at the clock. "Dr. Howard will be by later, I'm sure."

Winston leaned back in his chair. "How is Tina? And where is she, by the way?"

"I gave her the morning off. Ha!" He flashed a silly grin at his joke. "No, she's fine. Worried, of course. Today, she is getting some things done at the house. She'll be back here tomorrow. So, what's happening in the real world?"

The door to Jonathan's room opened before anyone could answer the question, and in hobbled the speaker on crutches.

"Good morning, Jonathan." Seeing the men, she added, "And hello, gentlemen. I'll be brief. I'm released, heading home!"

Jonathan smiled. "That's wonderful! Oh, these are the gentlemen I mentioned I wanted you to meet. Frank Osborne and Bartholomew Winston."

Frank and Winston, already on their feet, walked over and introduced themselves.

The speaker shook Winston's hand. "Very pleased to see you again. It's a shame that, throughout all my visits to the White House, we never had the time for more than just a hello. Congratulations on your retirement a few months ago."

Winston bowed his head slightly. "Thank you, Madam Speaker, and I'm happy that you are well enough and able to go home."

The speaker looked at Frank. "Mr. Osborne, it's an honor to meet you. We've never met, but I've read about your career. Very impressive."

Frank beamed and thanked the speaker, adding, "It's my honor to finally meet you."

The speaker, struggling a bit to maintain a comfortable balance on her crutches, looked at Jonathan. "Hon, when do you expect to be out of here?"

Jonathan made a face. "Soon, I hope!"

"Not soon enough." Her eyes scanned over Jonathan's two visitors. "Nice meeting you gentlemen." She blew a kiss to Jonathan, maneuvered her crutches while Frank held the door open, and then exited the room.

Frank gave Jonathan a mock-shocked look. "Wow, that's nice. How many people get kisses blown to them from the Speaker of the House?!"

Jonathan shrugged. "She and I have talked a lot over the past couple of weeks, and I have to admit, I really like her. Turns out, she and I have an equal loathing for President Elizabeth Gentry."

Winston shook his head. "I believe we all may be equal in that regard."

"I would only admit this to you two, but I'm telling ya, I actually am surprised by my level of hate for Gentry." Jonathan stared straight ahead and then continued. "I just cannot stand the thought that she's still in office. I actually am losing sleep over it."

Frank grabbed the briefcase he'd set beside his chair and placed it in his lap. "Jonathan, here's the first draft of the articles of impeachment. I believe we have more than what will be needed for House and Senate support."

Jonathan lifted the document, feeling its weight. "This is heavy!"

"There are seven charges, by the way," Frank chimed in. "Nixon only had three."

"Thanks for bringing me the draft. It's good to have it. Gives us a sense of accomplishment," praised Jonathan. "I look forward to reading it over the weekend."

Winston stood. "I'm heading up to Philadelphia this afternoon for a few days."

"Nice. Any special plans?" Jonathan inquired.

"Well, tonight I'm cooking, so a quiet dinner in front of the fire. Tomorrow, we'll be in front of the TV watching the Eagles/Ravens game. Turns out Beverly is a big Eagles fan, and, well, the Ravens are my team, so this should be a good test of our relationship." Winston smiled.

Frank nodded. "Should be a great game."

"No doubt," seconded Winston. "And on Monday, we're seeing the Matisse exhibit at the Philadelphia Museum of Art."

Jonathan sighed. "I look forward to when Tina and I can do things like that."

Frank grinned. "Jonathan, it's all possible. The key ingredient is retirement!"

. . .

It was late afternoon when Dr. Howard, seated near Jonathan's bed, had run through everything he had to tell his patient.

Dr. Howard finished with, "To summarize, your test results were good, and I am in agreement with the doctors: The trigger, here, for such a severe event was likely the metabolic changes due to you abruptly stopping your Metformin prescription. We'll spend the next several days closely monitoring you, and you need to let me know of any issues. Any questions?"

"Just one." Jonathan leaned forward. "When can I get out of here?"

Dr. Howard smiled. "Depends, of course, on your physical therapy, and more importantly, how your cognitive performance progresses. My best guess is you may be with us for another seven to ten days."

Jonathan nodded, though he couldn't help but feel a stab of disappointment. "Darn, that's a long time, but I understand."

Chapter 24

Wednesday, November 25
Thanksgiving Eve
The White House

The East Room was filled to capacity; the three eight-hundred-pound chandeliers with their one thousand crystal lights shined their brightest, and the stadium-like press lights only amplified the effect.

The TV monitors showed the sixteen-by-twenty-foot stage with its edge bordered by two-foot-high ferns. President Gentry, clad in a dark brown wool pants suit, stood next to the chief justice of the Supreme Court. At exactly 10 a.m., the oath of office for Georgia governor and now vice-presidential nominee, Celine Johnson was administered.

As soon as the words "I do" left the VP's mouth, the chief justice and vice president shook hands. The president moved in as the chief justice stood back, and the two hundred standing guests loudly applauded as Gentry and Johnson clasped hands. After a long handshake, the president, followed by her new VP, left the stage, waving to the onlookers. They exited into the Green Room, where an usher closed the door behind them.

President Gentry immediately stopped walking and swiveled to face her vice president. "That went well. I've got to go up to the private residence to take care of something. Go ahead over to your office in the Old Executive Office Building, and we'll catch up later."

Vice President Johnson smiled. "Madam President, thank you for everything."

President Gentry gave a sharp nod. "Of course. I'm looking forward to how we're going to win Georgia. Talk to you soon." With that, the president left the room, accompanied by her chief of staff, Wendy Wolf.

Once inside the elevator with the doors closed, the president said to Wendy, "I'm glad that little ordeal is over with. I sure hope our experts were right, and this will ensure we win all the southern primaries."

Wendy smiled reassuringly. "I have no doubt we'll win them easily."

The doors opened to the private residence, and the two got off the elevator together.

"The real reason we came up here is I didn't want to have to walk with the vice president. But while we're up here, let's have some coffee and go over some things."

They settled into two plush chairs in the West Sitting Hall, and the president pushed the button for the butler, who appeared almost immediately and offered a courteous greeting to both women.

"Nathan, bring us two coffees. Thank you."

Nathan nodded and left the room.

The president now faced Wendy. "Okay, what's next?"

Wendy glanced at the iPad in her lap. "Believe it or not, you don't have anything until a four o'clock taping of your Thanksgiving message to the troops. Tomorrow, your schedule is clear. Friday morning, you are having tea with the Chinese ambassador and Harvard professor, Dr. Zhang."

The president's expression soured. "Oh, damn. Are they going to ask me about their request to move a portion of that Chinese porcelain exhibit from the New York Metropolitan Museum of Art to the White House China Room?"

"That may come up, yes."

Gentry blew air through her lips. "How about we let the Smithsonian give them space? Let's have them deal with this."

"Remember, you're going to be the first president since Nixon to improve relations. This means a lot to the Chinese leadership. It would go a long way if you were the one to personally accept. Plus, this is a lot easier than taking pandas."

Gentry sighed dramatically. "Okay. Make sure the White House curator is on standby. I may want to bring him in just to make it look like I'm serious about this."

Seconds later, Nathan brought in a silver tray with a coffee pot and placed it on a small table. He deftly poured two coffees and served them.

Gentry, ignoring Nathan, asked, "Okay, Wendy, what else?"

Wendy scanned her screen. "Nothing. Oh, reminder: Tomorrow is Thanksgiving. Your husband, Admiral Curtis, is arriving home from his Middle East peace negotiations and will be here in time for your four o'clock dinner."

Gentry rubbed her forehead. "Shit. Please have someone else here with me. I can't bear the thought of a long dinner alone with him."

Wendy offered a sly smile. "Maybe I can get the vice president to join you."

"Cute, Wendy. Cute."

"Actually, Roman Mirov and his wife, Claire, will be here tomorrow afternoon, and they're overnighting in the Lincoln Bedroom."

The president brightened. "Oh, that's right. Great! Thanks for the reminder—looking forward to seeing them."

Chapter 25

Wednesday, November 25
Thanksgiving Eve
Paris, Virginia

Sunset was scheduled to arrive at 4:42 p.m. At 4:30 sharp, the large, black Chevy Suburban pulled into Jonathan and Tina's driveway.

A male nurse, with the aid of the two FBI agents, slowly guided Jonathan from the vehicle. Tina walked ahead and opened the garage door. The men helped Jonathan to stand, then he immediately asked for his crutches, insisting on walking the rest of the way on his own. Slowly, he maneuvered around the vehicle and into the garage. As he focused on getting to the door, he couldn't help but notice his mangled bike on the floor nearby, one of his bike shoes still attached to the pedal clip.

Overcome by a great sense of accomplishment and relief, he sunk into his comfortable living room recliner and exhaled. The nurse brought him a water bottle and asked if there was anything he needed. Jonathan smiled and, after drinking his water, mentioned that he might need help standing in order to get to the bathroom.

. . .

Tina began preparing dinner while the nurse sat at the kitchen table, using his laptop. Jonathan had fallen asleep in his recliner. Meanwhile, two agents, stationed in Jonathan's driveway, sat in their vehicle, exchanging chitchat while intermittently surveying the area.

The doorbell rang, waking up Jonathan.

Jonathan grabbed the walky-talky and yelled, "Tina, don't open it until I check!" After Jonathan clicked to the right channel, the agent in the Suburban immediately responded.

"Yes, sir. Sorry, we didn't have time to give you a heads-up. All's good. It's Sam Poundstone, plus one."

Jonathan's shoulders slumped in relief. "Roger that." As he placed the radio on the table, he called, "Tina, it's okay. It's Sam Poundstone."

Tina opened the door and gave Sam a warm hug, then hugged Greg Leidner. "Come on in, guys—so good to see both of you. I'm relieved you're here. Let me take you to him."

Sam Poundstone walked into the living room first. He was an imposing figure, nearly as wide as he was tall, a former Navy SEAL who had spent twenty-two years in the Secret Service as the lead for the emergency response team. He then worked a half-dozen years for Interpol until age fifty-five, when he retired from that position, moving on to undercover intelligence in Moscow and Istanbul. Sam then moved to the West Coast where, for the past several years, he'd been in Santa Monica running a very successful business providing security services to the rich and famous.

Greg Leidner, also a big man at six-foot-four, not to mention muscular, popular, witty, and gregarious, had risen through the ranks of the Secret Service and retired seven months ago, when he joined Sam on the West Coast as his right hand.

Jonathan wore a big smile at the sight of his two friends. "Pardon me for not getting up, but it sure is great to see you two. Sam, man! You look chiseled, buddy. You must be working out every day! To what do we owe this wonderful surprise?"

Sam responded, "Jonathan, I wanted to be out here much earlier. I sent Greg in advance so he could see you last week."

Jonathan nodded. "I hope you can stay the night."

"We were planning on it!" replied Sam.

Jonathan's smile faltered. "Uh-oh. This isn't just a friendly visit?"

"Oh, we're planning to enjoy it," Sam assured, "but as you've already figured out, we got some intel. So, we thought this might be a good time to come by and celebrate Thanksgiving with you."

Tina, standing in the doorway, chimed in, "Honey, there's more. I have a little surprise—Winston, Frank, and Brent will also be joining us tomorrow for Thanksgiving."

Jonathan grinned. "Fabulous! Wow, this will be great!" Already, he felt like his dreadful stay in the hospital—and hopefully, his memory lapses along with it—were drifting far into the past. Better times seemed ahead.

Chapter 26

Thursday, November 26
Thanksgiving
Capitol Hill, Washington, DC

Sylvie awoke to her phone ringing and answered.

The speaker's voice was loud and cheery on the other end. "Good morning! Sylvie, I just had a great idea—since you're French, you bring the wine."

Sylvie sat up in bed, blinking to clear out the morning cobwebs. "Uh, sure. I can do that."

"Don't forget to bring your Congressional ID. My security detail will need to see it when you arrive. See you at two o'clock!" The phone went dead.

Sylvie had just dropped her business phone on the table, wondering where she'd find a place open at that hour, when her personal phone rang. She pulled the phone out of her purse, which sat next to the bed, and checked the ID. It was Roman Mirov. Sylvie cleared her throat and hit the Talk button. "Good morning, Roman. Happy Thanksgiving!"

Roman with a thick laugh said, "You sound like an American!"

Sylvie winced at the insult. "Stop."

"Ha! I just wanted to check in on you. I hope you're not going to be stuck in your apartment all day."

"No, I thought I told you—the speaker invited me for dinner. Hey, I need your help. Where can I find a good wine store that would be open today?"

Roman answered immediately. "MacArthur Beverages off MacArthur Boulevard, upper northwest DC. The place is magnificent and open today."

Sylvie breathed out a sigh of relief. "Perfect. Thanks."

Roman went on, "I received a report that Jonathan Cartwright was released from the hospital and is now at his home in Paris, Virginia. Be aware—we have some assets monitoring his activity. I have authorized them that if the opportunity presents itself, they are to eliminate him."

Sylvie cocked her head. "Good, this will be one less headache."

"Oh, I forgot to tell you about your man, Karl Popov. He's thirty-eight years old, single, an American citizen but born in Russia. His father used to be a very wealthy man, but he made some bad investments and died under mysterious circumstances. Popov came to the US when he was twenty. He attended Ohio State, played two years of ice hockey. At twenty-one, he got into a little trouble and was arrested for assaulting a woman, but his record was expunged. I'm trying to get more details on that. Five years ago, he was charged with sexual assault, but the charge got dropped. He has had a variety of jobs. These days, he considers himself a lobbyist. I'm trying to find which members of Congress he's close to, but I haven't been able to determine anything yet."

Sylvie absorbed all of that. "Thanks, all good to know. He struck me as a real loser."

"Okay. So, unless something comes up, I will report back to you in a couple of days. Claire and I are spending Thanksgiving at the White House."

Sylvie grinned. "Well, well, well, aren't you and I covering all the US leadership?!"

. . .

Sylvie was thirty minutes late and likely the last to arrive at the quaint 1906 three-story brick colonial on A Street NE on Capitol Hill. Her tardiness was a side effect of her jaunt all the way to upper Northwest DC to get three bottles of Saint-Émilion. After showing her ID to the Capitol Police, she had walked the additional ten steps to the front door and knocked; seconds later, Derek Monet opened the door and, with a big smile, said, "Happy Thanksgiving."

Sylvie returned the smile. "Hi, Derek. I wasn't expecting to see you here." Sylvie stepped into the foyer.

Derek closed the door. "Oh, we do this every year!" He led Sylvie to the living room, where she joined the speaker and Jennifer; a nice fire was burning in the fireplace, and the nearby TV had a football game on, its sound turned way down.

The speaker looked up. "Welcome, Sylvie. So happy to have you join us, and I'm even happier that you brought the wine!"

Jennifer walked over and hugged Sylvie. She took the wine, then headed back to the kitchen, motioning for Sylvie to follow while telling the speaker to remain seated.

Sylvie glanced at the speaker, hovering in place for a moment. "How are you feeling?"

The speaker leaned back in her chair. "I'm fine, mostly because no one allows me to do anything!"

Sylvie smiled, then turned and rushed to catch up to Jennifer. Sylvie, before leaving the room, looked back. "Well, someone has been working hard. It smells wonderful."

"It's been a team effort, with Derek performing the master chef duties," the speaker told them from across the room.

Jennifer and Sylvie entered the large, modern kitchen, where Jennifer grabbed an ornate bottle opener and set to work on the wine cork. Derek joined them in the kitchen and tended to the turkey.

Sylvie watched the two of them for a moment. "So, you all have been doing this for years."

Jennifer twisted the gleaming corkscrew into the cork's center. "Well, it's only been five years for Derek. Suzanne—ah, excuse me, the speaker—and I have been doing this for over ten years. Hey, we're all single with no nearby family, and we have fun together, so we do holidays together."

"That's really nice, and I feel privileged to be part of it this year," Sylvie said, enjoying the warmth in the air, the feel of camaraderie, closeness, and family.

Jennifer, in a near whisper, revealed, "Yeah, the speaker really likes you."

Not long afterward, Jennifer, Derek, and Sylvie reentered the living room to find the speaker in tears.

Jennifer and Derek immediately rushed over to console her while Sylvie stood back, surprised and unsure what to do.

The speaker wiped tears off her carefully made-up face. Somehow, her mascara hadn't run yet. "My apologies, this happens on holidays. Even after all these years, I still miss my family so much. My little girl would be a grown woman now and maybe even have children of her own." She then put her head in her hands, released a few more sobs, then shuddered, exuding what was clearly a herculean effort to stop the tears. She looked up, eyes red and glistening, and offered a watery smile. "I'm fine, really."

Jennifer knelt closer to the speaker and put her young hands on the speaker's older ones. "We love you, we care for you, and we will always be with you during holidays…as long as you can put up with us."

The speaker's smile widened. "Thank you. You're so sweet…" She sniffled. "I'm fortunate to have you here, and this year is made even more special by Sylvie being able to join us."

Sylvie, hands clasped in front of her, watched the emotional scene play out. Softly, she said, "I feel very special to be here."

Jennifer moved back slightly, and Derek leaned in, placing his hand on one of the speaker's. The speaker seemed to absorb his warmth and compassion as if gaining strength from them, then, after a moment, said, "Thank you two. Both of you are wonderful. But can we eat now?"

They all laughed, then got down to the business of enjoying the holiday.

Chapter 27

Thursday, November 26
Thanksgiving
Paris, Virginia

As Winston helped Tina in the kitchen, both could hear roars of laughter coming from the living room.

Tina, salting the main dish, said, "Winston, thanks so much for being here. This is so good for Jonathan. He hasn't laughed like this in over a year."

"I wouldn't miss this for the world." Winston stirred the mashed potatoes a bit more. "That should do it." He set down the spoon. "I'm telling ya, these are gonna be great."

Tina nodded. "I'm sorry Beverly couldn't be here with you."

"We talked about it, and with this being her first Thanksgiving without her husband, we both agreed it would probably be best that she enjoy time with her daughter." Winston smiled, then added, "Maybe next year."

"That makes perfect sense." Tina dried her hands, then set the dish towel on the counter near the sink. "Let's get some wine and rejoin the fun."

. . .

After all were seated at the dining room table, Jonathan asked Winston if he could say the blessing.

Winston looked around the table; Jonathan, the nurse, Tina, Sam, Brent, and Greg all stared back at him. Winston took a breath, then began, "Lord God, our hearts are full of gratitude as we celebrate the feast of Thanksgiving. We are thankful for this gathering, and we wish for the safety and health of everyone at this table and those outside protecting us. We pause now and, in silent prayer, thank you for the great generosity of your gifts." After a pause, Winston finished, "Amen."

"Amen," voiced everyone else.

Jonathan held up his wine glass. "I would like to propose a toast. Please raise your glasses." Everyone obliged, and Jonathan looked around the table. "This is an amazing moment, to have all seven of us here. It means everything to me." Jonathan's voice cracked with emotion. "Here's to us and a good year ahead. Happy Thanksgiving!"

• • •

As the platters were passed around the table for second helpings, Sam leaned close to Tina and said, "Hey, I think I'm going to take a couple of plates out to the guys in the driveway."

Tina smiled. "Wonderful idea. I'll help prepare them."

"Perfect. Let's cover them in foil just in case they're busy."

• • •

As Sam approached the dark-colored van, the side door opened, and two young FBI agents smiled as they gratefully reached for the plates.

Agent One, a heavyset male, said, "Wow, Sam, so thoughtful of you to think of us. Come on in, have a seat. We'll give you the status."

Inside the van, the two agents placed their plates of food on a table, then took seats on small stools adjacent to a counter that contained a variety of electronic equipment and monitors.

Agent One went on, "We've been continuously scanning an eight- to ten-mile radius. It's been dead quiet all day—that is, until ten minutes ago when we picked up some radio activity heading west on Route 50 from Middelburg. The vehicle is traveling at or below the speed limit and just made a stop at Upperville, which is 4.5 miles from us. They're communicating with another vehicle to the south, which we tracked as they got off I-66. They're now heading north on Highway 17. That vehicle is now stopped approximately four miles from here."

Sam immediately straightened. "Okay, we planned for this. I'm alerting Mount Weather." Sam took his phone from his pocket and dialed the watch commander at Mount Weather. "Yes, this is Poundstone. I'm at the Cartwrights. We're preparing for possible assault. We have two FBI onsite, plus one of my agents and me. Please aid. What do you have available that can be here ASAP?"

The watch commander immediately answered, "Yes, Sam. I always have twelve rapid-response commandos on standby and can spare six to your location. ETA ten minutes."

"Please order that, and then contact state and local police and sheriff departments. Inform them of possible federal law enforcement activity involving FBI and Mount Weather and for them to stay clear of the area of Paris near Route 50 and Highway 17, Cartwright residence. We will contact them once the situation has been resolved."

"10-4. Stand by."

Sam waited on the line. Two minutes later, the commander continued, "Ordered. My men will be there in eight minutes. I also have two drones to give us some eyes. Have your agents work directly with my Ops team. I just texted you the number. Keep me informed. Commander out."

Sam ended the call, forwarded the information to the FBI agents in the van, then pocketed his phone. He glanced at the two agents who had since donned headphones and were hunched over their equipment. "What's the latest?"

Agent One answered without looking up. "No movement, but constant encrypted communications."

Sam frowned. "Mount Weather is launching two drones to help us. I just texted you the Mount Weather operations team contact info. Get online with them now." Sam glanced out the van's window. "It's 4:30. Sunset is in twenty-one minutes. I think they'll attack when it starts getting dark, probably between 5:15 and 5:30. I'm going back in the house for a few minutes." Sam opened the door to the van and started to climb out. "Call me if you detect any movement."

. . .

Sam entered the dining room to find everyone still at the table enjoying apple pie. Sam stood next to Jonathan at the head of the table. "Folks, we've detected some activity, and as a precaution, I'm going to have you move to Jonathan's very comfortable safe room." All the smiles quickly turned to solemn stares. "Let's move downstairs. Jonathan, don't worry. We'll carry you if we have to."

Everyone slowly began to move; the male nurse helped Jonathan.

Sam added, "Hoping this won't be long, but it may be a good idea for everyone to use the restroom, it's close quarters down there. Greg and I will get some snacks from the kitchen."

As soon as Sam and Greg walked into the kitchen, Sam turned to his friend. "Greg, I want you to get everyone settled, then leave the safe room, make sure they lock the door, and then join me outside in the FBI van."

Chapter 28

Thursday, November 26
Thanksgiving
The White House

Inside the family dining room, a fire crackled in the fireplace, and the table was formally set for the four guests. The butlers had just completed serving the turkey dinner to the president, her husband, and their two guests, Claire and Roman Mirov.

Admiral Curtis held up his glass. "I would like to toast my wife and our wonderful friends. Happy Thanksgiving."

All took a drink of the Louis Latour Puligny-Montrachet 2021 that filled their glasses, then began eating.

President Gentry smacked her lips. "This wine is perfect with the turkey."

Roman, his gleaming fork close to his mouth, met her gaze and held it. "I'm so glad you like it." His lips parted in a soft smile. "It came highly recommended to me."

Claire, in her very southern accent, chimed in, "Oh, Beth, it's so thoughtful of you to include us. Everything is so wonderful."

Gentry's eyes flashed to the woman. "Claire, I don't know that I would want it any other way." Again, facing Roman and catching his glinting eyes, she asked casually, "So, what are your thoughts on my VP selection?"

Roman's smile broadened. "I think it was a brilliant selection, and since we're friends, I'll tell you this— she will help you win Georgia, and maybe even Alabama, and she'll never get in your way."

"Exactly, Roman." Gentry looked pleased. "This is why I selected her."

"I want to share with you that Claire and I will be making a nice contribution to your election PAC." He examined his glass idly as if this was the kind of transaction people made every day. "I will transfer the funds tomorrow."

The president smiled.

Chapter 29

Thursday, November 26
Thanksgiving
Paris, Virginia

It was 5:15 and starting to get dark.

Sam and Greg stood outside of the van, talking to the agents through the open door. "Let's test our comms," Sam suggested, then pressed his earpiece closer to his ear and pressed a button on his sleeve. "Radio check, testing. Thumbs up if you hear me clearly."

The three other men gave a thumbs-up.

Sam faced the FBI agents. "Okay. You two, stay with the van. We have four Mount Weather troops in the woods near the end of the driveway, and the other two are behind the house. Greg, you stay near the front of the house. I will be roaming. Let's hope these new XM5 rifles handle as well out here as they did for us on the range last month."

Greg slid on his combat helmet, then grabbed his rifle and admired it. "Yeah, these are pretty damn spectacular—"

One of the FBI agents interrupted from inside the van. "We have movement." Both agents peered down at the monitors, watching the drones' live feeds. "Looks like two dark Mercedes SUVs heading this way well under the speed limit," the same agent said. "Infrared signature indicates three individuals in the car to the east, and four in the car coming from the south. ETA, five minutes."

Sam switched channels on his radio, sharing the updated information with the Mount Weather team. Then, he waited.

. . .

The 14×14-foot windowless room was sparsely furnished, with a worktable against the far wall. A half dozen folding chairs were stacked in the corner, and several large comfortable-looking blankets were stored on a metal shelf. In another corner of the room stood a refrigerator and next to it a small counter supporting a microwave oven. The dark and dreary 1970s paneling covered all the walls. The large florescent ceiling light provided adequate illumination. The dropdown ceiling was barely eight feet from the floor, making it feel claustrophobic. A small closet-sized bathroom was also part of the room.

A recliner was brought in, and Jonathan immediately sat and put his legs up. Others made themselves comfortable, some in chairs while others sat on the floor with blankets.

Winston looked around. "I never knew you had this room."

Jonathan chuckled. "It's not something I typically share with folks. But when we moved out here, the Department of Justice insisted that I have a 'safe room.' It's built with its own air and water purification system and has a separate power source. They say I can survive in here for thirty days." He shrugged. "Not sure how many days with all of us in here."

Tina added, "Yes, it's nice, but I still think it's creepy."

"Jonathan, please tell me that you have a bottle of single malt hidden in here," begged Frank.

Everyone laughed.

Brent was next to speak. "Is there any way to communicate to the outside from in here?"

Jonathan raised an eyebrow. "Actually, yes. Do you know Morse code?"

Brent's eyes widened a bit. "I have actually used that."

Winston looked at the nurse, eyeing him thoughtfully. "So, what do you have there, an earpiece?"

The nurse, seeming startled to be the center of attention, blinked. "Oh, this?" He raised his hand to his ear. "Yes, Sam gave it to me so I could monitor what's happening outside. Right now, nothing much. They're all just sitting in the van talking."

Jonathan crossed his arms and waited, unsure of how long they would need to remain in the silent, hidden room.

Chapter 30

Thursday, November 26
Thanksgiving
Paris, Virginia

Sam was standing halfway down the length of the thousand-foot driveway when he looked up. He spotted it before he heard it—the flash of a rocket as it flew by. He turned to follow its path just in time to see it impact and explode into the FBI van; a giant fireball emerged above the target. Sam immediately began a sprint toward the van. The sound and percussion of the blast almost knocked him off his feet. He regained his balance in mid-step and kept running. The van was totally engulfed in a raging flame. At fifty feet away, he could feel the searing heat and was forced to stop. Finally, he doubled over, hands on his knees as he gulped for air. Looking up, he realized there was nothing he could do; the agents could not have survived. Sam looked one hundred feet past the burning remains of the van to see Greg on the ground, struggling to get up.

Sam rushed around what was left of the van. "Greg! Greg! Can you hear me?" Greg appeared to be in a daze. Sam helped him up to one knee and looked him over, not finding any obvious injuries. "Greg! Greg!"

Greg looked at Sam and managed to hoarsely answer, "Yeah, Sam. Give me a minute. My ears are ringing. I'm having trouble…"

Sam swung his head around as machine gunfire could be heard near the entrance to the driveway. He pulled Greg up to a standing position. "C'mon, bud, I've got to get you to a safer spot." Sam led a wobbly Greg along as fast as he could to just inside the garage, where he sat him down against the wall and handed Greg his rifle. "Stay here. Defend the house!"

Sam got up to leave, then glanced back at Greg, whose eyelids were starting to droop, and yelled, "I need you to stay awake!" He then ran toward the gunfire, passing the van, which was still aflame. Once he was no longer illuminated by the fire of the burning van, he slowed to a half-jog. More shots rang out at the end of the driveway. He was maybe three-quarters the way down the driveway when shots shattered the silence behind him. *Most likely from the rear of the house*, he thought.

Then Sam heard footsteps coming toward him; he ducked behind the closest tree and waited. Two men approached, standing even with his location, just ten feet away. He could see they were not Mount Weather commandos but members of the attacking militia.

Sam raised his weapon, spun toward the men, and aimed. His first shot hit the closest one, going through his ear canal; he was dead before he hit the ground. Sam's second shot was so quick, the target never had a chance to react to his partner being shot. The bullet pierced his neck. He dropped like a rock but was still alive when Sam got to him. The dying man made a futile attempt at pulling out his handgun, but Sam was quicker; he pulled out his Sig Sauer and shot him between the eyes.

Sam sprinted to the end of the driveway, where he found all four of the Mount Weather commandos down. A quick check revealed they had been shot multiple times, but thanks to their level-four bulletproof Kevlar, they were still alive, though trying to regain consciousness after suffering from the equivalent of a hard kick from a horse. He noticed the militia SUV parked on the opposite side of the road, but where was the third militiaman?

As Sam headed back down the driveway en route to the back of the house, he radioed Mount Weather, reporting the location of the four downed commandos and that the injuries they'd suffered did not look life-threatening.

Approaching the house, another shot could be heard, this one from close to the house. Sam ran to the garage to find Greg still seated at the same location with a militiaman laying in a pool of blood less than ten feet from him. Sam got to Greg. "You okay?"

Greg gazed up with foggy eyes. "I'm good. I was just sitting here, trying to regain my senses. When I opened my eyes, that guy was coming my way. He must've thought I was dead, but surprise! Damn nice gun, by the way."

Sam looked around. "Okay, we got the three from the first SUV. Now we've gotta find the others."

Greg pointed behind Sam, who turned to see the two Mount Weather commandos who had been posted in the backyard.

One of the commandos reported, "We got two of the four, but the other two got away. We followed them but couldn't get to them before they drove off."

Sam nodded, then glanced down at his friend. "Greg, are you good to walk?"

Greg slowly got to his feet. "Oh, yeah. Not as spacey, so I'm fine."

"Let's patrol around the exterior of the house before we go inside," Sam instructed.

. . .

In the safe room, everyone was on edge after hearing the explosion and gunfire. Tina was laying in the recliner very close to Jonathan. He could feel her trembling.

Jonathan looked at the nurse who was seated on the floor in front of him, holding a cupped hand over his ear.

"What are you hearing?" asked Jonathan. When the nurse failed to respond, he yelled, "I said, what are you hearing?!"

The nurse held up a finger, indicating for him to wait. Then, the man casually reached into his medical bag and pulled out an automatic pistol. He pointed it right at Jonathan's head. "I am the last option," he told Jonathan with an eerie calm. "We thought of everything. This mission will not fail."

Jonathan shot a glance at Winston, who was seated closest to the nurse, then stared at the nurse and said in a very low voice, "Don't you know that everything here is recorded?" Jonathan briefly looked up at the ceiling.

Still pointing the gun at Jonathan, the nurse looked up for a split second. The punch from Winston hit the nurse's jaw so hard, he fell to the side, dropping the gun, which Brent immediately grabbed.

Winston jumped on top of the nurse while Frank pulled an extension cord out of the wall and used it to tie the nurse's hands behind his back.

Winston held his sore knuckles. "I never thought being a Marine Golden Gloves boxing champ would pay off fifty-two years later!"

There was a loud knock at the door. Everyone froze; then, they heard, "It's me, Sam."

Chapter 31

Friday, November 27
Paris, Virginia

It was shortly after midnight; two Blackhawk helicopters circled above the Cartwright property, while on the ground, dozens of FBI, Mount Weather, local law enforcement, and emergency medical personnel were working the scene.

Near the burned-out van wreckage, Sam and Jonathan, leaning hard on his crutches, spoke with the director of the FBI and the Mount Weather watch commander, plus several other senior officials.

The seasoned veteran FBI director spoke with emotion and said, "We lost two of our finest. This is a very tragic day in the history of the FBI. We have five enemy dead and are searching for the other two. We've ID'd them—all highly trained militia from West Virginia. We're familiar with them. They have long criminal records. We're questioning the nurse now and should have something to share in the next few hours."

The Mount Weather watch commander, who stood next to the FBI director, chimed in, "We have four men in serious condition, but they will recover. The militia was armed with Russian AK-308 field rifles."

The FBI director faced Jonathan. "Jonathan, I conferred with the attorney general. We are moving you and Tina to a safehouse in Pennsylvania. We have a team of eight special agents that will be onsite by the time you get there. Sam has agreed to join you up there later today. The chopper is on its way. Be prepared to leave in twenty minutes."

Jonathan nodded, shaking his head as if trying to dislodge the death and carnage around him. "Thank you. I'm going to head back into the house."

"Oh, Jonathan, I should add, you will also be accompanied by a medical team of two physician assistants, also trained as agents," the FBI director said.

. . .

Sylvie awoke to the sound of her personal cell phone; it took a moment for her eyes to focus. It was a text from Roman Mirov: *03:11am Mission failed Cartwright alive.*

Chapter 32

Friday, November 27
Capitol Hill

It was a few minutes past 7 a.m. Sylvie sat at her desk, large coffee in hand as she stared at her screen.

Jennifer walked through the open door of Sylvie's office. "Good morning! Have you been watching CNN? That militia attack in Virginia, near Mount Weather, is crazy." Jennifer stood next to Sylvie's desk and looked toward the TV.

Sylvie, searching for the remote, muttered, "No, I was finishing up my Euro trade report for the speaker." Finally finding the device under a stack of papers, she pointed it at the TV and turned-on CNN. They both watched.

A CNN reporter spoke into the camera. "…FBI and local law enforcement are not commenting other than to say the attorney general will hold a press conference at 11 a.m. CNN has learned through sources that it is believed a local militia led the attack on the private home. We do not have confirmation, but earlier reports indicated two agents of the FBI were injured during the attack. CNN has not been able to confirm why the FBI was on sight. A check of local property records revealed the home is believed to be owned by the Department of Justice, Office of Intelligence Director Jonathan Cartwright. No word on if Director Cartwright was at the location when the attack occurred. The closest neighbor, about a mile away, reported at around 5:30 p.m. hearing a loud explosion, followed by sporadic automatic gunfire, which lasted about twenty minutes. This was later followed by several Mount Weather vehicles arriving and helicopters flying over the scene."

The camera feed switched to the CNN studio, where Wolf Blitzer reported, "CNN is now able to confirm two FBI special agents were killed during the attack. Repeat, we can now confirm that two members of the FBI were killed. CNN is working to confirm reports that several members of the attacking militia were killed. We also have reports of several other casualties."

Sylvie muted the TV. "This is horrible."

Jennifer looked away. "It really is. The speaker is getting intel on this as well. Turns out, it was quite an operation. Oh, she wants us to have lunch with her in her office at 1 p.m."

"Perfect. I'll be able to deliver my final draft of the report to you by noon, and if you approve it, then you can give it to her."

Jennifer looked back at Sylvie as she left the office. "Sounds like a plan. See you at 1:00."

. . .

The speaker, Jennifer, and Sylvie all sat at a round table in the speaker's small dining room, which was part of the speaker's suite.

Suzanne spread her hands, indicating the dishes on the table. "I hope you guys don't mind; we're having Thanksgiving leftovers."

Jennifer smiled. "Oh, great. I loved everything the first time around!"

"Oh, yes, it was so good," seconded Sylvie. "Thank you for including me. My first time celebrating Thanksgiving!"

"We loved having you," assured the speaker. "Okay, ladies, my housekeeper packed this for us. Hopefully, there's plenty."

Jennifer unfolded an embroidered napkin and draped it across her lap. "So, what's the latest with the militia attack in Virginia?"

The speaker cocked her head. "Without being in a SCIF, there really isn't much I can share, but I can tell you, we now know that militia was not operating on their own. I talked to Jonathan. He and his wife, Tina, are fine but pretty shaken by this."

. . .

Sylvie greeted Roman and took a seat next to him at the bar. The Russia House Restaurant was practically empty at 2:30 p.m. on a Monday afternoon.

Sylvie leaned her elbows on the bar counter, looking askance at her comrade. "So, what's the urgency?"

"The Thanksgiving night attack failed miserably," admitted Mirov with a dour look. "Cartwright escaped without a scratch. He's now in a secure location, and we're unable to find him. Despite this failure, we've been authorized to eliminate the attorney general."

Sylvie did her best to qualm her frustration over this news. "I hope you made it very clear to Command that I had nothing to do with that preposterous plan of using an undisciplined militia to kill Cartwright. If I had been in charge, we would be having a very different conversation right now!"

Mirov was quick to console her. "I totally agree. I made it clear that Command's attempt of planning and executing a mission without my participation and their decision to use North Korean intelligence was a complete failure. As you know, Command never admits its mistakes. However, for whatever reason, in this situation, they did. Senior leadership even stated that neglecting to involve us was a serious error. And you should know, as a result, this has forced the immediate restructure of Command." Mirov took a swallow of his iced vodka, then continued, "They are asking for our strategy regarding the attorney general. I promised them we would have a solid plan within seventy-two hours and will be able to implement immediately once we're given the go-ahead."

"Good. I'll get to work on it immediately." Sylvie, in no mood to chitchat with Roman, added, "I've got work to do in the office, so I'm leaving." She then left as swiftly as she had entered.

Chapter 33

Friday, November 27
The White House

Harvard professor, Dr. Zhang, along with the Chinese ambassador stood as President Elizabeth Gentry, followed by the White House curator, entered the China Room. In the far corner of the room stood a table with the exhibits the Chinese ambassador had brought to show President Gentry.

President Gentry offered a big smile. "Mr. Ambassador, it's nice to see you."

The ambassador bowed, shook hands with the president, then spoke. "Madam President, it gives me great pleasure to introduce you to the esteemed Dr. Zhang, the world's greatest expert on the history of porcelain. Dr. Zhang is also the first cousin of our leader, Xi Jinping."

Professor Zhang bowed and, after shaking Gentry's hand, said in perfect English, "Madam President, it is the honor of a lifetime to meet you."

President Gentry pointed them toward two lavish chairs in the room. "Gentlemen, please be seated. I have asked the White House curator, William 'Bill' Adams, to join us." Bill nodded, and the president continued, "How amazing is it that we're meeting in the China Room of the White House?" The president looked at the curator. "Bill, please provide these gentlemen the history of this room."

The curator straightened and, with a proud look, began: "The China Room was established by Mrs. Woodrow Wilson in 1917 to provide a designated area to display the increasing collection of White House china. Practically each former president has samples of their china in this room. The collection is arranged chronologically, beginning to the right of the fireplace. Even the earliest presidents received government funds to purchase china. Early on, a clause in the budget appropriation bills included the verbiage: 'decayed furnishings.' This allowed for former presidential china to be sold and the proceeds to be used to buy new china.

As such, during the nineteenth century, the china sold at auction."

As he finished his well-rehearsed lecture, four butlers appeared with the tea service, which they placed on the table between the two pairs who sat in chairs facing each other, then poured and served cups of tea to each of the participants.

The Chinese ambassador smiled. "Madam President and Mr. Bill Adams, as you may know, for the past year, the Chinese have had the wonderful opportunity to work with the New York Metropolitan Museum of Art, which has agreed to display one of our larger collections of historic Chinese ceramics dating from the Kangxi period [1662–1722], one of the most productive periods of ceramics. Emperor Kangxi was the fourth emperor of the Qing dynasty and ruled for the longest period of any Chinese emperor."

The ambassador, seeming just as proud of his historic knowledge as had been the curator, walked to the table filled with exhibits and pointed to the blue-and-white vase. "The highlight of the collection we brought today is this eighteen-inch, blue-and-white 'figural' baluster vase, over four hundred years old and valued at over $250,000."

Dr. Zhang then stood and invited Gentry to take a closer look at the beautiful vase.

The president stared at it with an appropriate amount of reverence, remarked how much she liked the vase, and then invited Bill to take a closer look.

President Gentry then continued, "Mr. Ambassador and Dr. Zhang, I am so impressed with your presentation and these magnificent works that I agree to host this portion of your exhibit here in the China Room, under one condition." Everyone waited in anticipation. The president's eyes glinted a little—as if she enjoyed holding them in suspense—then continued: "That you allow me to have this amazingly beautiful baluster vase upstairs in the private residence, perhaps in the West Sitting Hall, where it can be enjoyed by my guests and me all the time."

Dr. Zhang beamed. "Madam President, nothing could please us more. My country will take this as a most significant step forward in a wonderful, warm, and long-standing relationship."

Bill examined the vase closely, then remarked for all to hear, "This is truly a remarkable piece. We will take great care of it."

"Bill, please take it upstairs and find the best location to place it in the West Sitting Hall," directed Gentry. "After tea, I will be taking the ambassador and Dr. Zhang to see it."

Bill nodded, donned a pair of white gloves, and carefully carried the vase out of the room.

Outside in the hallway, he encountered the president's chief of staff and told her, "Wendy, call the Secret Service TSD [Technical Security Division]. They need to examine this immediately. Have them meet me in the West Sitting Hall."

Wendy responded, "I'm on it!"

· · ·

Four minutes later, three TSD agents were using their flora scopes to carefully scan the vase.

One of the agents looked up. "Bill, we're done here. All's good."

"Excellent, thanks." With that, Bill escorted the TSD team out, then headed back toward the China Room, where he told Wendy all was fine. The vase was cleared.

Chapter 34

Tuesday, December 1
Manns Choice, Pennsylvania

Jonathan, Winston, and Tina sat in front of the fireplace; the large, bright-orange fire was doing a great job of keeping them warm. Outside, Sam Poundstone and ten Army Rangers patrolled the four-hundred-plus-acre property in the Allegheny Mountains. The light snow had ended, leaving less than two inches of accumulation behind. Five more Army Rangers were seated on the porch under portable heaters. In the driveway sat two large military RV command centers with large microwave antennas on their roofs that extended above the trees.

Frank Osborne had been in the kitchen a while, making grilled ham and cheese sandwiches and tomato soup. Finally, he stepped into the great room facing the fireplace and announced, "Guys, come on into the dining room. Sandwiches are ready."

The four sat around the table and were soon joined by Sam, who had come in from outdoors, removed his hat and heavy coat and took the remaining available seat at the table.

"This looks great." Sam settled into his chair and rubbed his hands together. "It's bitter cold out there."

Jonathan took a sip of his creamy tomato soup. "They say we may get six inches of snow tonight."

Tina hadn't touched the food in front of her. Stiffly, she looked up, her face a bit pale. "Sam, now that we've been here a few days, please again convince me that we are safe…?"

Sam nodded. "Yes. Not only are you well protected by fifteen elite-class Army Rangers, but I've also got members of my team here." Sam shifted his seat so that he was directly facing Tina, then continued, "We are monitoring the airwaves, we have the entire perimeter under electronic watch, and this entire region is on twenty-four-seven Department of Defense drone surveillance. Plus, less than one hundred yards away, in that field—you can see through the kitchen window behind you—we have two camouflaged Blackhawk helicopters waiting. And, finally, we have two RG-31 Chargers on the property. You are safer here than the president is at Camp David!"

Tina seemed to relax slightly. "Good to know. Hopefully, I'll be able to sleep tonight."

Jonathan frowned, troubled by his wife's fear and the uncertainty that now plagued his future. "So, where the heck are we?"

Sam answered, "We're ninety miles east of Pittsburgh, in West Central Pennsylvania, in the southern Allegheny Mountains, pretty much in the middle of nowhere."

Winston looked at his old friend. "Jonathan, so, what's next?"

Jonathan straightened, taking control of the conversation's direction. "I've arranged for us to meet the Speaker of the House, here, this week."

Tina jumped a little. "Oh my, we're going to need some groceries."

Jonathan put a hand on her shoulder. "The FBI will be delivering items this afternoon, but I don't want you worrying about the speaker. Winston has offered the use of a former White House chef, and the FBI will be providing all the food items that will be needed."

"Those two RV command centers in the driveway can each sleep six, so the Rangers will be completely independent from the house," Sam informed Jonathan and Tina. "Although, know that at all times, there will be at least ten of them patrolling the grounds, and they're well camouflaged, so you probably won't see them!"

Winston glanced around the room. "Where's Greg?"

"He's twelve miles away in the nearby town of Bedford," explained Sam. "He's just checking things out. He'll be on and off the property here, but his main job is to monitor and surveil the surrounding area." Sam left the room, poured himself a cup of coffee in the kitchen, then walked back toward the table. "Jonathan, as I showed you the night you arrived, you have a gun cabinet in your bedroom, equipped with two Remington 870 12-gauge pump shotguns, a Winchester model 94 30-30 scoped rifle, and two Sig Sauer P210 pistols."

Jonathan rubbed his chin and nodded. "That sounds perfect."

Winston commented, "Uh, no. Perfect would be if we were riding our bikes in Pacific Grove, California!"

Jonathan laughed, then was all business again. "Okay. Winston and Frank, let's spend some time planning for our meeting with the speaker. We will be discussing the Blake assassination report, and while I know she read it, there are several areas I need to emphasize. We also need to come up with what outcomes can be expected by the release of this report."

Chapter 35

Tuesday, December 1
Michael's Drive, Bethesda, MD

Delun Li sat in his basement recreation room, along with Dr. Zhang and three technicians. All five men wore headphones, listening intently to the highlights of the past seventy-two hours of recordings, which had been taken from the baluster vase now prominently located in the West Sitting Hall of the private residence at the White House. The vase contained the latest breakthrough in Chinese advanced technology: a sophisticated surveillance device using undetectable ceramic elements that picked up conversations up to a twenty-foot radius.

Delun finally lifted off his headphones, and the other four men immediately followed suit.

The lead technician spoke: "What you just listened to was a composite of the past few days. Our team continues to live-monitor twenty-four-seven. If anything else of significance comes up, the two of you will be notified immediately."

Delun smiled faintly. "I cannot believe our good fortune at the president insisting on having one of the vases in the private quarters. This will give us a tremendous advantage."

Dr. Zhang grinned. "We were so surprised. And she was so happy to have it, she invited the ambassador and me to see it once it was in place upstairs."

Delun ran a hand through his immaculately cut, short dark hair. "The only thing of significance we've learned thus far is that she has had two phone conversations with who we believe to be her Russian contact, Roman Mirov. Our analysis of the DOJ's Blake assassination report revealed that Mirov and the president communicate often via burner phones. Once we figure out how to monitor those phones, we'll be able to see the text messages and monitor both ends of their voice calls."

"This is excellent progress," agreed Zhang. "My cousin would like to see your plan, including a timeline on when we replace the Russians."

Delun stood and invited Dr. Zhang to join him upstairs for tea, then looked at the three technicians. "Gentlemen, excellent work. Thank you for the report. We're going to leave you now. Please continue your monitoring and let me know what you may need. Help yourselves to anything in the kitchen. I have a HelloFresh delivery coming this afternoon. You're going to love the meals I picked out. Are your sleeping arrangements good for you down here?"

The lead technician responded, "Yes, sir. This is luxury compared to our last assignment on a submarine."

The men laughed as Delun and Dr. Zhang left the room.

In the kitchen, as Delun prepared the tea, he remarked to Zhang, "I've just received confirmation from what we learned from our informant, a Russian named Karl Popov. He shared that the speaker's new French staffer, Sylvie Bardot, is really Russian Agent Annika Antonov. Antonov is a highly trained FSB agent who has been involved in numerous assassinations, including the murder of former President Blake last March. The Americans believe she was shot dead by Department of Justice Agent Jonathan Cartwright."

Dr. Zhang's eyes widened. "This is remarkable. We need to learn what her current assignment is."

"That shouldn't be too difficult." Delun poured the tea into a small, ornamental cup. "She reports to Roman Mirov. We'll be able to determine her activities based on our ability to listen in on President Gentry's communications with Mirov." He handed the cup to the doctor.

He took it and sipped the tea, wearing a pleased expression. "Excellent. Before I report to my cousin, I need to know your planned timing of when we will be replacing the Russians."

Delun's often unreadable expression clouded for just an instant before hardening back into stone. "Yes. You have made that clear. I will have that plan completed very soon. I believe our best method of takeover will be to fully comprehend President Gentry's thoughts on what her priorities are for eliminations, and we will step in to handle those while ensuring our presence is known to the president. What

241

better way to gain President Gentry's confidence in us, especially since the Russians have failed miserably with their last few assignments!"

Dr. Zhang nodded. "Perfect, my cousin will be very pleased."

Chapter 36

Wednesday, December 2
Capitol Hill

The Washington, DC Eastern High School choir finished the final crescendo of their resounding version of "It's Beginning to Look a Lot Like Christmas." The speaker, on crutches, stood at the podium in front of the fifty-five-foot tall, twenty-five-foot-wide Engelmann spruce from Colorado. Maneuvering a bit gingerly, the speaker slowly swiveled about, thanking the choir, several dignitaries, and finally, various members of Congress who were present. She then announced to the crowd of several hundred on the west side of the Capitol, "Let's count down! Five…four… three…two…one!"

Instantly, thousands of colorful lights illuminated the majestic tree. The Army band lifted their instruments. The melodic notes of "O Christmas Tree" filled the massive space, to the delight of the audience.

Sylvie and Jennifer, having stopped for drinks at Bullfeathers, arrived just in time to see the tree illuminate. Now, standing amid the large crowd, the air cool, crisp, and filled with Christmas music, they were really feeling the spirit of the season.

"That was nice," commented Sylvie, eyes on the brilliant spectacle of the tree. "So, what now?"

"You get to go home while I have to go with the speaker to have her sign several committee actions," Jennifer told her with a sigh.

Sylvie frowned. "Oh, I'm sorry you have to deal with that. But I am exhausted, and an early night would be ideal."

Jennifer nudged her. "Yes, dear, go on. Let's have breakfast tomorrow, bright and early." Jennifer looked ahead; she could see the speaker just twenty-five feet away, surrounded by admirers, and as she started to head in that direction, she looked back at Sylvie with a smile. "This is what I do best—free her from the throngs!" And off she went.

Sylvie scanned the surroundings with a quick, trained eye and thought she caught a glimpse of Karl Popov in the crowd. Anxious to avoid the man, she plotted her route home. Quickly, she freed herself from the masses and began her walk home down the quiet and dimly lit circle drive on the south side of the Capitol. She made a left onto Independence Avenue and headed east. Ten minutes later, as she approached 3rd Street, her sensible shoes leaving little sound to distract her, she sensed she was being followed. She made a quick decision: Rather than go all the way to her apartment at 4th Street SE, she made a right on 3rd and headed away from her place.

Moments later, she saw a shadow turn and follow her. Though it was dark, she could tell it was a large man, maybe fifty feet behind her. She made a right onto D Street SE, and suddenly, he was even with her. Sylvie, surprised at her stalker's speed, almost raised her fists to engage him. She immediately calmed slightly. It was Karl Popov.

Popov, walking swiftly, his motions deft and surprisingly nimble, grinned. "Sylvie. I didn't mean to startle you." As he got close—a little too close, in

Sylvie's opinion—he casually mentioned, "I was hoping to have heard from you. How is it going?"

Sylvie, annoyed and not hiding it, answered, "I'm fine, Popov. I don't appreciate being stalked."

Popov jabbed a finger across the street. "This is Folger Park, one of my favorite places. Let's take a walk in the park." It sounded less like a request and more like a demand.

Sylvie frowned, glancing ahead. "Not now. I'm exhausted. I need to get home."

"But your place is a few blocks in the other direction," Popov reminded her.

Sylvie's eyes swung over to meet his. "How do you know where my place is?"

"I've been researching you. Did you not know I'm Russian? So now, let's go for a little walk together." Popov took Sylvie by the elbow and escorted her, none too gently, across the street and into the park.

The park was dark. They were alone.

Sylvie's mind moved through the options of how best to play this out. She decided to feign ignorance. "What does your being Russian have to do with anything?"

"I know who you are, and don't worry, your little secret is safe with me. I don't want money. I just would like for us to be friends…" He grinned. Even in the darkness, she could see his ugly intentions. "What is the expression? Friends with benefits?"

Sylvie pulled her arm away.

Popov was clearly irritated. "If you're nice to me, then I will help you," he hissed, then grabbed her and pulled her close, clamping his lips harshly on hers.

Sylvie pushed him away, stepping backward while she wiped her mouth.

Popov bared his teeth. "Okay, Ms. Annika Antonov, I think you would be wise to give in to me."

That stopped Sylvie in her tracks; he really did know who she was. She would have to rethink matters.

The punch was lightning-quick; Sylvie never saw it coming. His knuckles landed solidly on her forehead. She hit the ground hard, the wet grass slightly cushioning the fall.

He leaped on top of her using all of his six-foot-four, 270-pound frame, grabbing her arm and pinning it behind her as he tore off her jacket with his free hand and began ripping her blouse open.

In Popov's rush for gratification, he neglected to realize she still had full reign over one arm. She grabbed his hand and twisted two of his fingers into dislocation, hearing his bones cracking. Popov rolled off her in agony. Laying on his stomach, in severe pain, he tried to move his fingers back into place. Sylvie immediately straddled his back, grabbed his head in an armlock, and in one fluid motion, twisted and jerked his head to the left, snapping his neck. He went limp.

Sylvie dismounted the dead man, then got up and grabbed her jacket and purse, closely inspecting her surroundings for witnesses. Finding none, she pulled out her cell and texted Mirov: *Need large body disposed, pick up in Folger Park near corner of 3rd & D St SE.*

Mirov's response was immediate: *Got it, ETA less than 10 minutes, leave scene NOW!*

Seven minutes later, Sylvie, from a full block away, watched from the corner of North Carolina and 4th Street SE, where she had a clear view back to the scene. She did not have to wait there long before she spotted the dark van that pulled up. Two men in black got out, dragged over the body, then loaded it into the van and sped off.

She took a deep breath, smoothed her jacket, and then calmly walked the remaining two blocks to her apartment.

Chapter 37

Thursday, December 3
Manns Choice, Pennsylvania

The H3 chopper kicked up snow as it landed. After a few minutes, the rotors stopped, the door opened, and the speaker emerged on crutches with the aid of two armed soldiers wearing camo. She was followed by Jennifer Largent. The soldiers helped the speaker and Jennifer get seated in an ATV and drove them the 150 yards to the large, A-frame house where Jonathan, Winston, and Frank awaited them.

Jonathan, standing on the side porch on crutches, greeted her. "Welcome, Madam Speaker."

She groaned and yelled over from the open door of the vehicle, "Oh, Jonathan, stop that shit and call me Suzanne. That goes for all you boys!"

Suzanne, intent on moving without help, shooed away the two soldiers standing on either side of her and, with a lot of effort, got out of the ATV. With surprising speed, considering she was using crutches, she maneuvered to the porch to join the others. Jennifer, carrying several bags, struggled to keep pace.

"Hi, all," Suzanne said with a smile and a few beads of perspiration on her forehead. "And for those that haven't met my wonderful chief of staff, this is Jennifer."

Jennifer gave them a warm smile.

Frank said, "C'mon in. We've got a nice fire blazing, and I just made a batch of hot chocolate."

Everyone entered the house and was immediately appreciative of the warm fire.

"Grab a seat in the living room," invited Jonathan. "Then, after we've warmed up, we'll move to the dining room table for our meeting."

Suzanne glanced around. "Beautiful place you have here, Jonathan."

Jonathan answered with a smirk, "Why, thank you, but this belongs to a guy we all know, our Uncle Sam."

This brought a few laughs from the group.

. . .

Once all were seated around the large dining room table, Jonathan handed out copies of the slide deck to Suzanne, Jennifer, Winston, Greg, and Frank. "This is the latest version of my Blake assassination report. It goes into great detail on the specific areas I am recommending for a future federal grand jury to look at."

For the next two and a half hours, the group reviewed the details of the Blake assassination and the specific areas in which they recommended indicting the president.

After the group had finished, Jonathan spoke. "To conclude, we've laid out seven indictable offenses: failure to preserve, protect, and defend the Constitution of the United States; violation of the oath of office; obstruction of justice; abuse of power; contempt of Congress; conspiracy to defraud the United States; and tax fraud." He paused. "Of course, it really will fall under the purview of Congress and/or the federal grand jury as to what may end up being the specific charges against the president."

Suzanne mulled that over. "My concern with Congressional hearings is that they can take over a year. A grand jury, on the other hand, can easily take eight or fewer months. That may be the logical way to go. We really can't let this drag out. Gentry needs to be impeached and removed before she commits irrevocable harm."

Frank argued, "Don't you believe, with the overwhelming evidence we have gathered, that if presented in the proper fashion, the House could vote for impeachment, and the Senate would uphold it?"

Suzanne sighed. "Yes, that may make the most sense. I'm pretty sure I can deliver the House, but the Senate is a completely different animal. How about if Jennifer and I work up an approach? I can run it by someone in the Senate leadership that I trust, and maybe we can come up with a successful strategy." Suzanne looked at Jennifer. "Let's have a draft in a week that we can all approve."

Jennifer nodded. "I will adjust your schedule as necessary to ensure we have the time this task will require."

Suzanne smiled. "Perfect."

"Outstanding work, Jonathan," praised Winston. "Your report clearly implicates the president and Roman Mirov, but can we be certain there aren't others involved in this?"

Jonathan looked thoughtful. "Good point. I don't have proof yet, but by proximity, the president's chief of staff, Wendy Wolf, must know something."

Winston mentioned sarcastically, "Well, as Gentry's polling numbers indicate, she is indeed amazing, but in all seriousness, I have to believe she's getting help from somewhere."

"You may be right." Jonathan slowly leaned back in his chair, eyes sweeping all the table's occupants. "Which leads me to other concerns I'd like to discuss with the group."

Suzanne gave a wave. "Please, go on."

"As I've shared with the group, I'm concerned that the attorney general and possibly others have been compromised. I sent my final draft of the assassination report to the attorney general, who said he never received it. I've pointedly asked him about this twice, and he told me twice, in very convincing terms, that he'd never seen it. So, I had the classified IT folks check it out. They reported it to cyber security, whose investigation revealed that the report was successfully sent and successfully received by the AG, who opened it on his classified workstation in his office, and that the next day, it was deleted. What I have not shared with anyone is that the cyber folks determined that my email was also opened at an internal DOJ IP address belonging to someone on the IT helpdesk, who has since been arrested and has lawyered up—they're not talking. So, we can't be certain who may have a copy of my report."

Winston's eyebrows raised. "Wow."

Frank seconded with, "Holy shit!"

Suzanne grimaced. "Yeah, what he said!"

Jonathan scrubbed his face with his hand. "Something's going on here, and it isn't good."

"Does cyber have any theories?" inquired Frank.

Jonathan smiled slightly. "Actually, they do and have requested I meet with them tomorrow."

Suzanne's face had turned grave. "Please keep me informed."

"Absolutely."

Suzanne reached over and grabbed the crutches leaning against the side of her chair. "Well, gents, I think we've had a very productive time here today. I do need to get back to the Hill. Jennifer, what time is that vote?"

Jennifer checked her iPad, always kept within arm's reach. "It's scheduled for five but will most likely be at six. Right now, it's 3:10. Thanks to the US Army, our chopper should have you back in the office by 4:00."

"Perfect." She faced Jonathan. "Jonathan, I'm having a Christmas party for the leadership tomorrow at 6:00. There will be heavy hors d'oeuvres, and, of course, cocktails. I would like for you and Tina to please attend. I've also invited the attorney general." She flashed a sly grin. "Might provide a chance to have a private chat."

Jonathan's smile was just as sly. "Why, thank you. That sounds wonderful, as long as my security detail permits."

Suzanne answered with a wink, "Oh, they'll permit it. See you tomorrow."

Chapter 38

Friday, December 4
US Capitol Building, Washington, DC

Jonathan was managing remarkably well with his crutches as he and Tina got off the elevator near the speaker's office. Tina looked radiant in her dark blue Saks Chiara Boni La Petite long dress. As they headed toward the Speaker's Lobby, they could hear a choir singing carols and a lot of guests conversing. The Lobby, known for its portraits of past Speakers of the US House of Representatives and located just outside the east end of the House floor, was where a lot of the real business of Congress took place between its members. The Lobby contained the speaker's office and several cloakrooms, all connected by a corridor wide and long enough to host scores of people. Ornate, crystal chandeliers hung from the high ceiling.

Specially set up for the speaker's Christmas party, many chairs, settees, and tables currently lined the walls; the tables contained an appealing assortment of heavy hors d'oeuvres, including sliced beef tenderloin, large gulf shrimp, beef wellington bites, crab cakes with mango-avocado relish, and tuna tartar.

The speaker stood at the head of the hallway, greeting guests as they arrived. There must have been close to two hundred, and more were still coming in. Butlers stood by with trays of champagne. Tina grabbed one for Jonathan and herself as they passed.

The speaker warmly greeted Tina, complimenting her on her fabulous dress. She then hugged Jonathan and whispered in his ear, "Surprise, surprise. The president will be here tonight."

Jonathan rolled his eyes. "Oh, boy." He then looked the speaker up and down. "What? No crutches?"

The speaker leaning on her cane, "Yes, I'm trying to make it with just this, which, by the way, makes me look rather sophisticated, non?" She laughed.

As Jonathan and Tina mingled, a few members of Congress greeted Jonathan, offering their sincere concerns and condolences over the attack at his home.

Further along, Jonathan saw Jennifer and Sylvie, who both smiled and said their hellos.

Jonathan, weary from all the movement with his crutches, suggested to Tina that they find a seat somewhere. Tina led Jonathan to a comfortable seat and stood next to him.

The Senate majority leader soon approached Jonathan with a smile. "Good to see you again. I was very concerned over what you had to endure. We cannot allow those militia thugs to get away with this sort of thing." He turned his sympathetic smile in Tina's direction. "Are the two of you okay?"

Jonathan answered, "Thank you for your concern, Senator. We are fine… I should be off my crutches in a week or so, hopefully—"

The crowd's loud murmurs and shuffling stopped him in mid-sentence. They all turned to see what the commotion was about.

They got their answer soon enough. President Gentry and her entourage were entering the Hall. The senator smiled at Tina and Jonathan, nodded, then stepped away.

True to form, Gentry looked supremely elegant in her bright red Andrew Gn gown. Wendy Wolf accompanied her as they slowly made their way to the opposite end of the Hall, where the speaker was still greeting guests.

A few from the president's cabinet were also among the guests. Jonathan could see his boss, Attorney General Edward Stanton, speaking with William Brookhart, the chairman of the Judiciary Committee.

Tina brought Jonathan a plate of shrimp and another glass of Moet Chandon, both of which he took gratefully.

"Thanks, babe. I'm so glad I'm no longer on any meds." He sipped the bubbly concoction, which tickled his throat and immediately sent a shot of warmth into his stomach. "I can really enjoy this champagne."

Tina squinted at him. "That's your third glass. We don't want any crutches mishap, so that should be your last one."

Jonathan smiled. "Yes, nurse." He held up his glass to toast her.

Jennifer Largent approached Jonathan and leaned close to him to avoid any of the nearby guests overhearing. "Mr. Cartwright, the speaker requests your presence in her office, where she will be hosting an impromptu meeting with the president and the attorney general."

Jonathan put down his glass. "I'll be right there." Jennifer left, and Jonathan motioned for Tina to come closer. "I need my crutches. Big-time meeting in the Speaker's office. Take my seat. I'll be back as soon as I can."

Tina retrieved the crutches from the floor behind Jonathan's chair as he stood and motioned for Tina to take his seat. As she maneuvered to get by him, he kissed her on the cheek.

It took Jonathan a while to get through the throngs of guests. He looked ahead and could see the AG, followed by the president and then Wendy Wolf as they entered the speaker's office. Two minutes later, Jonathan managed to maneuver his way into the room. Jennifer closed the door behind him, and the speaker bid everyone to take a seat.

Gentry lifted her chin. "That won't be necessary. I am hoping this meeting will not take long. Madam Speaker, what is this about?"

Suzanne waved at Jonathan as if she hadn't heard the question. "President Gentry, I don't believe you know Jonathan Cartwright. He is—"

The president interrupted, "No, we have not met, but I am well aware of who he is. Why is he at this meeting? Aren't we here to discuss a matter with the attorney general?"

The speaker replied, "The matter we wish to discuss is the Blake assassination report. The report's author is Mr. Cartwright. We have concerns because the report was delivered through secure communications. However, the AG never received it.

We have reason to believe elements of the DOJ have been compromised, and by statute, once I have been made aware of such information, I am obligated to inform you. Tomorrow, I will inform the Judiciary Committee, who will likely open an investigation."

The president, confident the AG would disavow any reason for the president to be part of the meeting, turned to him with a steely stare. "Edward, do you have anything to offer on this?"

The attorney general's face was carefully neutral. "Madam President, as attorney general, I, too, have a sworn requirement to uphold and protect the constitution. Also, being the nation's chief law enforcement officer, I have duties I must enforce. And actually, I've already started working with the Judiciary Committee. The FBI has made two arrests for the theft of classified information. The fact of the matter is, I did receive the report, and my apologies to Mr. Cartwright."

The AG faced Jonathan and continued, "In order to not disrupt our investigation, I had to tell you that I never received the report." Edward turned back to the president. "Earlier tonight, I discussed this matter with the chair of the Judiciary Committee. He believes, if this can be resolved internally, then there will be no need for congressional or presidential involvement."

Gentry nodded, looking satisfied. "Edward, what is next regarding the report?"

"After our review, we'll determine what needs to be redacted for security purposes. Then, a redacted version will be released to the Congress and, ultimately, the public."

Gentry gave Suzanne a cold look. "Is there anything else that needs to be discussed here? Otherwise, Madam Speaker, I need the room for just a few minutes in order to confer with my attorney general."

The speaker, a bit taken aback, muttered, "Uh, I suppose we're done here, Madam President. The room is yours."

The president and AG remained standing as everyone else exited the room, the speaker being the last one out. She closed the door behind her.

The president waited all of thirty seconds before she started screaming, "What the fuck, Edward?! I'm surprised you didn't just point to me and say, she made me do it! I told you to *lose* the damn report!"

Edward retreated a step. "I didn't have much choice, given the fact that the cyber team and the inspector general had proof that I had received it. I used the excuse that my reasons for saying I never got it was part of a sting operation. We lucked out because we did find someone on the inside that had illegally obtained a copy. No one suspects you. I am the only one that knows the truth, and as for the actual report, we'll redact anything that shines a negative light on you."

Gentry, seeming slightly mollified, waved him away. "Edward, that will be all. You can go now."

The AG left the room.

. . .

Back at the White House, the president sat in the West Sitting Hall with a large snifter of cognac. She pulled out her private phone and called Roman Mirov.

Mirov answered, his words slurred as a result of having consumed several vodkas. "Good evening, Madam President."

The president made a disgusted face at her contact's current state but informed him, "Roman, I am forced to make this decision. Top priority—eliminate the AG. Let me be perfectly clear. This is a priority. Next, I need the speaker and then Jonathan Cartwright eliminated. No more mistakes. Make it happen." The line went dead.

Chapter 39

Saturday, December 5
US Capitol Building, Washington, DC

For the past two hours, the speaker, the AG, and Jonathan had reviewed the assassination report and discussed their plan to impeach the president.

Jennifer placed a carafe of coffee in the middle of the table. AG Edward Stanton was the first to reach for it. He refilled his cup, then filled Jonathan's while Jonathan watched him through narrowed eyes.

The speaker lifted her cup and saucer, a heavy look on her face. "Gentlemen, I really appreciate the two of you being here. I don't expect we'll be too much longer."

The AG nodded at her before turning toward Jonathan. "Jonathan, again, my apologies. I hated misleading you." He almost looked abashed.

The speaker's expression didn't soften. "Ed, you and I have worked well together, starting way back when you were judge on the US Court of Appeals for the DC Circuit. I have always admired and respected you and, above all, trusted you. We have reason to believe that President Gentry pressured you into 'losing' the report. Is there any truth to that?"

Edward picked up his coffee, staring down at his cup. "Suzanne, this is putting me in a no-win situation."

Suzanne leaned forward. "She's blackmailing you, isn't she? Ed, we will protect you!"

The attorney general didn't look up. "You don't understand," he said quietly. "There are some things that occurred in my background that I'm not too proud of. I just can't talk about it."

The speaker gently touched his arm. "If you will tell us what really happened, we'll help you. We'll come up with a plan."

The AG took a long breath. "Please give me some time to think all this through." He blinked hard, his mouth twitching a little. "Believe me, I want to do what's right."

Jonathan also leaned forward. "Ed, if it would be helpful, I am available to talk to you about it anytime."

Edward almost smiled. "Thanks, Jonathan. I'll think about it."

Jennifer burst into the speaker's office without knocking.

Suzanne looked up with an impatient expression. "What is it, Jennifer?"

Jennifer looked apologetic at the news she was about to deliver. "In two minutes, you are to address the Federal Technology Council in HC-4 [House Reception Room]. FYI, there are over three hundred attending. They're spilling out into the hallways!"

"Thanks, Jennifer." The speaker sighed and eyed the two men facing her. "Okay, gents, I need to go. We'll need more time for us. Jennifer will reach out to you and schedule something." Suzanne stood, grabbed a notebook, and headed out the door.

Jonathan, having finally swapped out his crutches for a cane, followed the AG out of the office and into the Speaker's Lobby, where they were met by a young man in a blue blazer, khakis, and a blue tie. "Gentlemen," the man intoned, "due to a Congressional event, I need to show you out. Please follow me."

They exited the Speaker's Lobby through a side door, which led to an elevator. Jonathan and the AG entered the elevator, and the young man pressed the button for L3.

Jonathan suddenly felt a bit of anxiety. Worried that he might be starting to experience another memory issue, he glanced at the back of the young man's head. "Where is my security detail?"

He answered, "I'm taking you to them."

Jonathan frowned. "Where?"

"Basement, lower level three. The tunnel level."

The elevator door opened; warm, damp air quickly filled the elevator. The young man swiftly exited to his right and disappeared down a dimly lit hallway. The

AG stepped off; Jonathan followed more slowly, cautiously looking down to place his cane.

The next thing Jonathan knew, his mouth was covered with tape while a hood came down over his head. His cane was snatched away, and he was kicked in the back of his legs, causing him to drop to his knees. Disoriented, he tried to stand but was forced down. His wrists were tied behind his back with what might have been a nylon fastener. Still on his knees, he could hear the AG not far from him, pleading, "No. Wait!"

Jonathan was startled by the sound of two muffled gunshots from what must have been a silencer, immediately followed by the thud of a body hitting the ground. He braced himself, believing he was next. Instead, he felt someone reach under his arms on either side of him, lift him to his feet, and force him to walk forward. It was uncomfortably warm and humid. Jonathan could tell he was walking on a damp surface as he could hear the moisture from his steps. His legs hurt since he had not totally recovered from the injuries of his attack five weeks earlier.

They walked for maybe ten minutes, making various turns along the way. Twice, his captors pushed his head down, Jonathan believed, to avoid some type of obstacle. Finally, they stopped. Jonathan was forced to sit on what felt like a wooden bench. His captors tied his legs to something. Then he felt a stinging sensation in his neck and heard them walk away. The entire time, they had never said a word; he blacked out.

. . .

The AG and Jonathan's security details were working with the US Capitol Police, conducting a room-by-room search as they fanned out from the speaker's Office. Some Congressional staff attending the Technology Council event were being questioned by law enforcement after having reported briefly seeing a House page escort the AG and a man with a cane.

Provided total access, and given the full endorsement of the speaker, Sam Poundstone and Greg Leidner arrived on the scene. They appeared combat-ready in their tan-colored camouflage and matching military utility caps. Both had an M18 Glock sidearm holstered. Sam received the latest status and update from his old friend, the chief of the Capitol Police, who had immediately strode up to Sam upon seeing him.

"Chief, have you had the witnesses review photos of all the Capitol pages?" Sam asked.

The chief replied, "That's being done now."

Sam nodded. "Good, be sure and let me know what they come up with."

Sam and Greg then met with the speaker and Jennifer Largent in the speaker's Office.

"Sam, thank you for getting here so quickly." The speaker looked weary and as if she had aged a few years since they last spoke. "I'm just sick to my stomach about this. It is outrageous. How is it possible that we can't find the AG or Jonathan?"

"We'll find them, ma'am," Sam assured. "Every exit to the complex has at least two Capitol Police officers using electronic facial recognition monitoring. Every person is being checked." Sam turned to Suzanne's chief of staff. "Jennifer, can you please escort us to the chief architect's office?"

Jennifer frowned. "It's Saturday. He probably isn't here."

"He's here," said the speaker. "I saw him earlier."

Jennifer led the way. "Let's go."

Jennifer, Sam, and Greg traveled the back halls, then walked into the reception area to the Architect's Office. Jennifer walked past the receptionist without even looking at her and opened the door to Derek Monet's office to find him at his computer.

A startled Monet looked up. "Oh, hi, Jennifer. I've been following the activity. What's the latest?"

Jennifer gave a quick wave to indicate her two companions. "Meet Sam Poundstone and Greg Leidner. They are law enforcement and experts in personal security. The speaker wants to ensure they get everything they need."

Derek stood. "Welcome, gentlemen. Please have a seat."

Sam took a seat across from Derek. "Thank you, Derek. Tell me—if you were going to hide someone in the Capitol complex, where would you do so?"

Derek gave an immediate response. "There is a series of underground steam and utility tunnels that encompass the entire campus. That's where they could be."

Sam straightened. "Take us there!"

Derek took off his suit jacket and carefully draped it over a chair. He then went to his closet, took a white lab coat off the hanger, and slipped it on. He grabbed a white construction helmet from the upper shelf and placed it on his head, then took three heavy-duty flashlights and handed them out. After grabbing a pair of construction boots from the closet floor and swapping them out for his wingtips, he took a six-pack of bottled water from his fridge and distributed the bottles.

Derek led Sam and Greg out of his office and told his receptionist that he would be in the tunnels where cell reception was nonexistent. Fortunately, the Capitol Police had lent Mr. Poundstone one of their radios, which, thanks to them having installed emergency transmitters years earlier, enabled them to receive comms and that she should contact the police for anything urgent. He looked back over his shoulder and told Jennifer he'd meet her in the speaker's Office when done.

They took an elevator to a basement level, then headed down a clean, well-lit hallway that ended at another elevator. The four of them got in, and Derek pressed the button for L3. The old elevator groaned as it moved slowly.

Derek explained, "We're going to start with a network of old utility tunnels that were built in 1908 to supply steam and electricity to the congressional office buildings and Library of Congress. Gents, these tunnels are cramped—only seven feet tall and 4.5 feet wide. The steam pipes make it difficult to get around, and the temperatures down here are around 100 degrees."

The elevator doors opened, and everyone immediately felt the heat.

Sam asked, "How far do we need to go?"

"We're at the midway point," replied Derek. "To the right, the tunnels head south to the southernmost point, which ends at the Capitol Power Plant. To the left, they go all the way to Union Station, which is the northernmost point. We'll start by heading south, and when we get to the end, we'll turn around and head all the way to the northernmost point, then walk back to here. We also will check the smaller tunnels that go to the individual buildings on Capitol Hill."

The men began walking. The passage was narrow, and the heat made it most uncomfortable.

"I'm already sweating like a pig, and it feels like these walls are closing in on us," said Greg nervously.

Sam frowned. "Just focus, Greg. Focus."

"I am." Greg looked down and shined his flashlight. "Yikes! Look at the size of that roach. It looks like a tortoise!"

Thirty minutes later, they reached the Capitol Power Plant.

"Derek, how long will it take us to get to Union Station?" asked Sam.

Derek answered, "At least an hour."

Sam pulled out the radio provided by the Capitol Police and pressed the button. "This is Poundstone. We're searching the utility tunnels. Any new developments above ground?"

A Capitol policeman responded through the heavy static, "Negatory, hold on. Chief reports the witnesses saw no matches on the photos of existing Congressional pages."

Sam replied, "10-4. Out." He took a long drink of his water, then said, "Let's get a move on."

. . .

After ninety minutes of searching the entire route and coming up with nothing, the men rode the elevator back up to where they had originally started. They were exhausted and soaking wet.

Sam faced Derek. "Okay, where next?"

"Follow me." Derek explained as they walked, "Our next set of tunnels is a bit shorter. Built in 1865, they would pack the inlets with ice to offer cool ventilation to the Capital Building to offer relief from the terrible summer heat. It actually worked! Later, as improvements were made, these tunnels were sealed at the ends; hence, why these, like the last set, will be warm and stuffy, but they are bigger—ten by ten feet. We'll start with the House tunnel. It's over two hundred feet long. There's a matching Senate tunnel, but that is mostly filled in now."

The doors to the elevator opened, and as the men stepped out, they were again hit by warm, humid air. They turned on their flashlights. Before them was a square ten-by-ten opening encased in rough concrete.

Derek led the men forward. Just a few steps outside the elevator, Sam yelled, "Stop!" He pointed his flashlight into the corner less than fifteen feet from where they stood. The others shined their lights to reveal something covered by an old canvas tarp.

Sam walked over and slowly pulled the tarp off. Two large rats scurried away. Sam stared at the body of the attorney general in a pool of blood. He could easily identify two 9mm-sized bullet holes in the AG's forehead; he checked for a pulse, knowing there would be none. He shook his head and took a few steps backward, lifting his radio. "This is Poundstone. I've recovered the AG's body. He's deceased, two gunshots to the forehead."

"Copy," the staticky voice replied through the radio. "Your location?"

Sam looked at Derek, who responded, "L3 old ventilation House tunnel."

Sam spoke into his radio, "We're in the L3 old House ventilation tunnel. The body is less than ten feet to the left when you get off the elevator."

"Copy that," said the policeman via the radio.

Sam pressed the button again and continued, "I'm here with the Architect, plus one of my men. We're moving on to search for Cartwright. Out." He placed his radio back on his belt and glanced at Greg and Derek. "Let's continue. It's going to get really crowded down here in a few minutes."

One hundred feet later, they ducked under a large support beam and continued. Their lights revealed several more rats running along the corridor. The damp, stagnant air made it difficult to breathe. To make matters worse, they were disappointed when their lights allowed them to see all the way to the far end of the tunnel. No sign of Jonathan.

Sam hissed out, "Damn."

They walked another ten feet.

Greg pointed. "Hey, look! Down there on the left. I think there's an opening to another tunnel."

Fifty feet later, they made a left and had to duck under another support beam. Twenty feet past that, their lights illuminated a hooded figure, slumped and seated on the right. The three men ran.

Sam got there first and yanked the hood off the man. "Jonathan, you're good!"

Jonathan blinked until he could clearly see the men.

"Hold on, bud. I've gotta pull this gaffer tape off your mouth," said Sam.

Derek held a water bottle for Jonathan to drink from while Sam used a knife to free his hands, then his legs.

"You okay?" Sam asked.

Jonathan nodded slowly. "A little groggy. They shot me up with something." He swallowed. "They killed Ed, didn't they?"

Sam frowned. "I'm afraid so."

"Two shots with a silencer?"

"Yes. Both to the forehead."

Jonathan snarled, "Dammit to hell! So, why am I still living?"

Sam frowned. "Maybe they figured you wouldn't survive down here for long."

"Or they were going to use me for ransom. Does Tina know about this?"

"No. I don't believe so," answered Sam.

"Good! Let's keep it that way."

Chapter 40

Monday, December 7
Russia House

It was close to 11 p.m. Sylvie and Roman Mirov sat at their normal spot at the end of the bar. Both were staring at their vodkas.

"So, explain this to me again," instructed Roman, eyes on his glass.

Sylvie took a breath and went through the details again. "I was sitting in the Speaker's reception room. My plan was to lead the AG to the speaker's elevator, the one she always used—the one without a camera. Being Saturday morning, no one was expected to be around the speaker's Office. However, down the hall, there was a large overflow reception. The AG and Jonathan Cartwright left the office. I followed several feet behind and was surprised when I got to the hallway and saw a House page. Before I could react, he got the AG and Jonathan Cartwright to follow him. The page took less than fifteen steps down the hallway. On the left, he held open a door for them. They walked through, and the page followed, closing the door behind them. I immediately reached for the door handle, but it was locked."

Roman glowered. "What happened next?"

"I went back to the office and asked an aide where that door led. They said they had no idea; they had never seen it open." Sylvie took her drink from the bar, absentmindedly sipped the vodka, then set it back down and continued, "A few hours later, news was spreading fast through the Capitol that the AG was missing. Soon, CNN and others were reporting it. No details have been released."

Roman signaled to the bartender that they wanted two more drinks. He then looked at Sylvie and thought out loud, "Well, this leaves us in a very strange predicament. The president ordered me to eliminate the AG, and the AG has been eliminated, only we didn't do it!"

"She also wants the speaker and Cartwright eliminated," Sylvia reminded him, then frowned, suddenly puzzled. "By the way, where is Cartwright?"

Chapter 41

Tuesday, December 8
The White House

President Gentry pressed the button on the side table in the West Sitting Hall, summoning the butler. Moments later, Nathan walked in.

"Yes, Mrs. President. What can I get you?"

"In ten minutes, I'm hosting a very prominent Harvard professor. He's Chinese, and I would like for tea to be served. Once the tea is served, I would like for you to leave the floor," she instructed.

"Yes, as you wish, Mrs. President." Nathan left to prepare the tea.

Gentry picked up the phone and waited for the admin operator to answer. "Get me the Ushers Office," she directed the operator.

"James Allen is on the line, ma'am."

Gentry launched into her instructions. "James, I'm hosting Professor Zhang for tea. Please call me when he arrives, and I'll give you the go-ahead on when to bring him up. Also, I don't want anyone else in the private residence while he's here, and be sure and mark the visit as OTR [off the record]."

James answered, "Yes, Mrs. President." The phone went dead.

. . .

The phone rang. The president answered and said, "Bring him up."

Gentry welcomed Dr. Zhang as he exited the elevator and invited him into the West Sitting Hall, directing him to a comfortable seat before settling into one near him. "Dr. Zhang, good to see you again, and thanks for coming on such short notice."

Dr. Zhang smiled. "It is my pleasure. Thank you for having me."

Nathan walked in with a silver tray with tea service for two. He placed the tray down on a table that sat between the two, then left and immediately returned with pastries.

Gentry never took her gaze off the professor, even as Nathan moved into her line of vision to arrange the pastries on the table. "Dr. Zhang, I believe that you and I can enjoy a very beneficial relationship." They both took a sip of their tea, and she continued, "I will be very honest with you. There are certain things I need and expect precision and expertise with. Unfortunately, as of late, I've experienced times where my tasks have not been completed to my satisfaction. I am sad to share that the existing arrangement I have is coming to an end."

Dr. Zhang nodded. "We only know one level, and that is perfection."

"Yes, I believe the manner in which you handled the attorney general is a very good start." She smiled. "I will begin to phase out my Russian associates and will involve you more in future endeavors."

Dr. Zhang sipped his tea. "Madam President, nothing could please us more."

Gentry continued, "I would like to see how you handle a very important assignment for me. I need to have the Speaker of the House eliminated. And if this is a success, I am prepared to provide some key relief to some of our harsher trade sanctions with your country. After which, other actions I initiate could well provide advantages to you."

"Thank you, Mrs. President. One of our priorities is to gain more information on your successful and very impressive nuclear submarine capabilities. Perhaps you would be in a position to assist us there."

Gentry sipped her tea. "I think you will find my rewards for your help are commensurate to the specific task I assign you. In other words, you help me, I help you."

Dr. Zhang nodded. "Perfect, Madam President, perfect. I believe, as you said earlier, we will enjoy a very beneficial relationship. As a matter of fact, we have already arranged for ample contributions from private investors. We are in the process of providing millions of dollars to your PAC. And no one will ever be able to trace it."

Gentry leaned back, looking quite pleased. "That's wonderful news, thank you."

The two went on sipping their tea and talking of nonessentials, now that the most important business was out of the way.

Chapter 42

Wednesday, December 9
Manns Choice, Pennsylvania

Jonathan put down his coffee cup and pulled up his schedule on his laptop. His next meeting was with his tech specialist, Tim, at 10 a.m. After lunch, he would be meeting with Winston and Frank. So, a pretty light day. He still had not told Tina about the prior Saturday's abduction, nor had she asked him about the persistent media reports of the AG having gone missing.

Jonathan looked up to see the flat-screen TV in the living room, which displayed the CNN Breaking News banner. He found the remote and turned up the volume just in time to hear Wolf Blitzer's report:

"CNN has just learned that Attorney General Edward Stanton was found dead from an apparent self-inflicted gunshot. There had been persistent rumors the past several days that Stanton had gone missing. We are now going live to CNN's Kasha Garrett, reporting from outside the Department of Justice."

Jonathan's pulse raced. Tina, having heard the TV, walked down from the upstairs bedroom. She was joined by Sam, who came in from the kitchen. They all focused on the youthful face of Garrett on the wall-mounted TV as she said, "Yes, Wolf, I am here outside the Robert F. Kennedy Building where details of the attorney general's tragic death are just starting to emerge. The DC medical examiner reports Stanton had suffered a gunshot wound to his temple. No further details have been made available. It is assumed that Assistant Attorney General Robert Blaylock will take over as attorney general. We've just been told that the Department of Justice will hold a press conference later this afternoon."

The screen switched to the control room, where Wolf Blitzer stood, talking into the camera. "Kasha, are there any indications of why Stanton would have taken his own life?"

Kasha answered, "Wolf, some close associates of Stanton are reporting that he had become quite despondent over the past several weeks. Some believed he was suffering from depression. No further details have emerged. Wolf, that's all I have at the moment. We'll undoubtedly learn more at this afternoon's press briefing."

The camera feed switched back to Wolf. "Edward Stanton was one of President Elizabeth Gentry's first cabinet appointments. He was confirmed by the Senate and sworn into office last March, just ten days after former President Blake had been assassinated. You are watching CNN's continuous coverage of the death of Attorney General Edward Stanton. We'll be back after the break with CNN White House Correspondent Haley Shear."

Jonathan muted the television, then looked at Tina and Sam and shook his head. All he could say was "This is bad."

Tina moved close and touched his arm. "I'm so sorry, hon. Did he have any family?"

Jonathan looked down. "He had a wife. They did not have any children."

Sam moved closer. "How's Blaylock to work with?"

Jonathan sighed and lifted his chin. He had to move forward. "He's good. I've worked with him on a few things. He's been around for a long time. Not so sure he and President Gentry will get along too well, which might actually be good."

An agent knocked at the door, interrupting their thoughts. The man stuck his head in, said good morning, and informed them that Jonathan's 10 a.m. appointment was being driven up to the cabin.

Jonathan stood and said to Tina and Sam, "Let's discuss this more later."

Sam grabbed his coat and headed out. Tina mentioned that she would be on the lower level working out if Jonathan needed her.

Jonathan, with the help of his cane, reached the door and welcomed Tim into the house. "Hey, Tim. How about some coffee?"

Tim waved away the gesture. "No, thanks. I had some on the drive up."

Once they had moved into the dining room and seated themselves at the table, Jonathan began. "What do we need to go over?"

Tim opened the laptop he'd set on the table and commenced typing. "I've got footage of two more Roman Mirov visits at Russia House."

"Okay, how many photos do I need to review?"

Tim replied, "We've got sixty-seven, but now that we have three recorded visits, we've used analytics and have prioritized visits to the same individuals that have been there during the times Mirov was there. So, with that, we only have eleven photos to view."

Jonathan nodded. "Great, let me see them."

Tim placed the laptop in front of Jonathan.

Jonathan stopped at the second image and squinted. "This was the one I noted last time. You didn't get anything on facial recognition?"

Tim leaned closer to the screen. "No, and strangely, she was the only one we didn't get a hit on."

Jonathan reviewed all eleven of the photos, then said, "Let me see what you have from the database on the others."

They spent the next thirty minutes going through the data.

Jonathan rubbed his forehead, thought for a moment. "Give me the digital images from number two—all three of the visits."

Tim nodded, his fingers deftly flying over the keys. "Okay, they're in your email."

"Good work, Tim. Thanks."

After spending just a few minutes reviewing the photos, Jonathan notified his security detail: "I need to get to the Capitol."

Chapter 43

Wednesday, December 9
US Capitol Building, Washington, DC

Jonathan sat in Derek Monet's office in a chair opposite the desk the architect now sat behind. "Derek, thank you for seeing me on such short notice. I have a classified matter I need to discuss with you, and I need you to agree to keep this just between you and I."

Derek nodded. "Of course."

Jonathan pulled his MacBook Air out of his bag, opened it up, positioned some photos for Derek to look at, then handed the computer to him. "I would like you to view these seven photos and let me know if you recognize the individual."

Derek, after just a few seconds, said with widened eyes, "Yes, I would say this is Sylvie Bardot, although I've never seen her in casual clothes. But, yeah, especially these two where she's not wearing a hat. I would bet it is her."

"Many thanks, Derek. That's all I needed."

. . .

Late afternoon.

Jonathan waited in a nearby vacant caucus room while the speaker was attending a Floor session. He was alone and really enjoying the tranquility and beauty of the room. He spent nearly two hours writing down his ideas for the best approach on how to handle Sylvie, given the new information he had.

His thoughts were interrupted when Jennifer walked in.

Jennifer offered a friendly smile. "Hi there! Suzanne is back and ready to see you."

Jonathan followed her down the hall and into the speaker's Office, where they found Suzanne seated on her sofa.

"Jonathan, my apologies for keeping you waiting. Nothing happens fast out there on the Floor."

"No problem." He glanced at Suzanne's chief of staff. "I would like for Jennifer to stay for this conversation."

Suzanne raised an eyebrow. "Of course."

Jennifer settled next to Suzanne on the sofa. Jonathan took a seat across from them and said, "Before I start, I've gotta ask about the AG. Where the hell did they come up with that suicide story? CNN made it sound like it happened in his office at the DOJ. What the heck?!"

Suzanne lifted both hands in a helpless gesture. "The White House stepped in and took over. They claimed since he was a member of the cabinet, it was their jurisdiction, and you know what? I stood far out of their way!"

Jonathan said with angst, "Make sure you document everything! This will be added to what we have already under number four on our list—abuse of power."

Suzanne said with a smug look, "I already thought of that. I also think we need to investigate President

Gentry's overall involvement. We may end up with an additional conspiracy charge."

"Yes! And it remains to be seen, but if Blaylock ends up as AG, that could be really good for our effort," remarked Jonathan.

"Absolutely." She gave him a shrewd look. "So, always good to see you, but you're not here about the AG, are you?"

"No. I needed to get your opinion on something." Jonathan handed Suzanne the laptop, and both women looked at the photos.

Jennifer gasped. "That's Sylvie. Where is this?"

Jonathan looked toward the speaker. "Suzanne?"

The speaker looked up. "Yes, I would say that's Sylvie. So, what does this mean?"

Jennifer, still focused on the photos, added, "Definitely her. I recognize that leather jacket, and I saw her wear that polo cap the other night during the Christmas tree lighting."

Jonathan took a deep breath. "By the way, I believe the photos are of Sylvie as well."

The speaker frowned. "Okay, Jonathan, you're starting to make me nervous. What are you about to tell us regarding our favorite employee?"

"It's a hypothesis at this point, but I'm usually right." He shrugged. "Well, actually, I'm always right."

The speaker gave him a look. "Go on."

"These photos were taken outside of Russia House Restaurant. We have been monitoring this place since the Blake assassination, and Sylvie's three late-evening visits the past four weeks have been while Russian Oligarch Roman Mirov has been there. As you know from the assassination report, he's the FSB leader that is in regular contact with the president. So, one visit would be a coincidence, two is a high probability of a contact of some type, and three visits means they are working together!"

The speaker's mouth formed a horrified "O." "Oh my God. What the hell does this mean?"

Jonathan answered simply, "It means the Russians have someone on the inside."

Jennifer finally spoke. "*What?!* I'm shocked." She shook her head, seeming dazed. "I mean, I cannot move. I don't know what to say. I really like her. We have a bond... I can't think straight."

The speaker slammed her fist down on the empty couch cushion. "We need to have her arrested!" She noticed Jonathan's placid expression. "Jonathan, what do we do?"

"Nothing."

"What do you mean, nothing?!" Suzanne exploded.

Jonathan lifted a hand. "Let's think. This could be an opportunity. We need to get her to work for us."

Jennifer looked from Jonathan's face to the speaker's. "What?! Like a double agent? You can't possibly be serious!"

"Actually, I'm very serious, and we prefer the term counterintelligence. This is a rare chance that could be of tremendous value to us. Of course, this would require significant preparation, suitability reviews, an evaluation, and, of course, approval at the highest levels of the Intelligence Community. There would be tremendous risk involved, but the reward has the potential to be significant. The key to any possible success is limiting those involved. We would be dealing in the highest levels of government security." Jonathan's face was calm but his words stern.

Suzanne stared hard at him. "This sounds crazy. But I have to admit, I'm a bit intrigued. I mean, if I can be of help in such an endeavor, I would like that."

"Wow," breathed Jennifer. "I don't know. All this is a bit overwhelming. It's a little too fast for me. Plus, it's really disturbing, and I have to admit, it scares the hell out of me."

Jonathan gave her a sympathetic look, but went on. "Please know, this is only the slightest of possibilities at this point. Understand, there are a number of steps that would need to take place before this can be a consideration. The number of people that would know about this is the three of us, including just one or possibly two at the highest level, and, of course, Sylvie."

Jonathan continued, "I will be completely honest with the two of you: The potential benefit to the United States cannot be measured, but it would be significant. While you will be appreciated by those of us in the trenches, the two of you will never receive any public acknowledgment. I can assure you, however, you would receive the most incredible support apparatus in existence, and there would also be undocumented benefits that would make it worth your time."

Suzanne crossed her arms. "Now that last part sounds a bit shady."

Jonathan replied, "I can assure you, it's not shady at all. I just can't get into any detail at this time."

"So, if we agree to help, what orientation and/or training will we need?" the speaker inquired.

Jonathan leaned back. "You have almost everything already, and that's the ability to communicate and relate. We will provide guidance on specific areas, but all in all, this will not be a heavy lift for you." Jonathan looked directly at Jennifer. "Jennifer, you are the closest to Sylvie. How do you think she would react if you both approached her?"

Jennifer seemed to tense. "It's hard to say. Although I feel we're close, I've never felt like she was trying to take advantage of me. I think she trusts me. I sure don't see how knowing me could have helped the Russians. I think we can all agree, she is exceptionally smart and has adapted well to everything we've thrown her way. But of course, if she's really a Russian spy, she's likely very good at masking her emotions."

Jonathan asked, "Has she shared anything personal or confidential with you?"

"She once mentioned how hard it was growing up. She was into track and field, and she told me how much pressure her father and coaches put on her, that she never really got to be a kid," Jennifer recalled.

Jonathan nodded approvingly. "That's good. Anything else?"

Jennifer shrugged. "Just girl talk."

Jonathan shook his head. "I don't know what that is. Please elaborate."

"One night at Bullfeathers she mentioned a tough end to a relationship from earlier this year, but she did not want to talk about it further."

Jonathan seemed to absorb that. "OK, that's probably not relevant, if you remember anything else, please let me know. Every little bit helps to understand her and how she might react to specific situations."

Suzanne chimed in, "By the way, there are only two people I completely trust in Washington. One, of course, is Jennifer. The other is Derek Monet. Since he has dealt with Sylvie, I would like to have him weigh in."

Jonathan rubbed his chin. "I went way out on a limb sharing this information with the two of you. Our probability of success goes down drastically by involving someone else. What value does he provide?"

The speaker pressed, "I don't believe you can fully appreciate Derek's worth. Not only is he an excellent judge of people, but I have also entrusted him with some of the most confidential information in the entire Congress. Derek's character, honesty, and reliability are beyond stellar. He's also plugged in, so to speak. He hears a lot and can let us know of any potential hazards, leaks, etc. I strongly recommend we include him."

Jonathan paused to think, then pulled out his iPhone and called the chief architect. "Hi Derek, it's Jonathan. I'm in the speaker's Office. Can you please join us?" Jonathan ended the call. "He's on his way."

Less than three minutes later, Derek was seated next to Jonathan, who spent the next twenty minutes reviewing all the evidence and explaining the evolving plan.

Derek took in everything. "I appreciate you including me on this, and, of course, I'll be of assistance in any way you need. I should mention, interestingly, when I met with Sylvie one on one for coffee, we talked about when she was at the Sorbonne. It turns out we overlapped a bit. She and I were there at the same time. I was in architecture and engineering; she was law. There was something I meant to follow up with her on—it seemed a little off. She mentioned an art and architecture class that she took. She talked about the professor. She remembered the dates, the room, and talked about some of the subject matter. I didn't mention this, but coincidently, I was quite familiar with the class. In fact, the university assigned me as a visiting professor. I taught it! The regular prof was there but observed me from a seat within the class. The class had over forty students. I can remember a lot of them, and she was not among them."

"Hmm, that is interesting and good to know," commented Jonathan. "I'll add it to the file."

Derek glanced at the office door. "I have something else I need to share that can never leave this room."

Suzanne waved him on. "Please, share."

"I was tipped off that the assassination report had been obtained and was being delivered to Chairman Brookhart of the Judiciary Committee. I intervened and redirected it to the speaker." He met Suzanne's gaze. "My apologies for not giving you a heads-up, but I sensed this was rather volatile, and the less said, the better."

Jonathan's eyes grew wide. "Oh my! How in the world did you get involved in this?"

Derek's eyes slid to his. "Jonathan, let me just say, if you knew the things I am privy to, you would be in awe."

Jonathan slowly nodded. "Wow, I obviously underestimated your value. We need to have a conversation. I'll schedule something." He stood, walked across the room, and looked out the window. "Here is how I see this moving forward. First thing is a proper project name. From this point forward, this effort will be known as Project Idokopas. Idokopas is the location of Russian President Putin's palace complex, where he plans some of his more sinister moves. What better name for our effort? I will get the necessary approvals and support for this operation."

Jonathan looked at the ladies, "Suzanne and Jennifer, you two will be front and center on this. Meaning, with proper guidance, you will recruit Sylvie and handle her assignments. Derek and I will have no clandestine-related contact with Sylvie, so she will not know anyone else is involved. Sylvie will understand that she still works for the speaker, but in addition to her regular duties, she will have some off-the-record assignments that primarily will include providing detailed information on Roman Mirov and the Russian plans, which she will basically observe and report on."

The speaker grinned. "So, we'll be sworn agents?"

Jonathan smiled faintly. "Something like that. The four of us will meet regularly to exchange information and make any and all modifications as needed."

"What needs to be done with our clearances?" the speaker inquired.

Jonathan waved at both women. "You and Jennifer are currently Top Secret/Sensitive Compartmented Information. You have every category except Q, which is nuclear, and that won't be required for this assignment. I believe Derek is good as well, although I just need to confirm his level. At the appropriate time, I will conduct the 'read-in' to the project, but that's mostly an administrative step. I'll be able to handle everything."

Suzanne glanced at her chief of staff. "Jennifer, are you willing to do this?"

Jennifer squirmed a little. "Uh, I need time to think. If I do this, I guess I'll go from an eleven-hour day to eighteen or more?"

Jonathan looked apologetic. "Hopefully, this will only be temporary, but yes, to be honest, for a while, it may be twenty-four-seven."

Suzanne leaned forward, seeming electrified by the opportunity. "So, how do we get her to 'join' us? Do we pay her? What if she says no? And even if she agrees, how do we know if she's really working for us?"

Jonathan had his answers ready. "We have a specific process, let's call it a series of 'tests' that we've used for agents. It involves some specific scenarios and expected results. As for payment, yes, we handle that too. It's all done in a way that can't be traced. These are the areas that are more on the side of the things that I directly manage. Bottom line: You and Jennifer will be the single interface with Sylvie. You will build the relationship and basically be her point of contact for everything, to include her regular Congressional work, and then, of course, on a parallel and classified track, you will issue the assignments from me. Sylvie is never to know there is anyone else on the US side other than the two of you."

Jennifer blinked a few times, then slowly nodded. "When do we start?"

"We already have," Jonathan informed the two women. "Welcome to Project Idokopas."

Chapter 44

Friday, December 11
Manns Choice, Pennsylvania

Jonathan worked to complete his plan, using the assumption that Sylvie was likely a lower-level asset in the Russian FSB, which he believed made her all the more perfect to recruit. Her initial assignments would involve providing info on her precise role, details on her current assignment, and a list of her recent accomplishments. She would also be asked to provide basic demographic information on Roman Mirov's organization; i.e., hierarchy, names, and locations of FSB personnel, their communication methods, etc. If the initial intel she provided was verified, the next phase would involve having Sylvie provide specific details on the Mirov organization's planned activities and schedule. Long-term, eventually, the plan would be for Sylvie to disrupt and/or sabotage Mirov's FSB activities.

Never used, but always available to him at a moment's notice, Jonathan's Office of Intelligence had just over four million in cash, a sum left over from various past efforts, some successful, others not so much. This was considered Intelligence Project Operations money; no record of it existed. It had been amassed over several years by a clever, undetected budget rounding error, making the cash untraceable. Jonathan's first order of business: determining the best way to routinely deliver a "stipend" to the speaker and another to Jennifer. He decided to start with a nominal amount, maybe just a few thousand dollars, telling both women to classify it as money for expenses. Over time, he would increase the amount and provide them with the flexibility to make payments to Sylvie.

Jonathan spent the next hours wrapping up all the details, then used a secure line to reach out to his counterpart at the CIA, Denzil Jacobson.

Denzil was career CIA and the head of the Intelligence division. He and Jonathan had spent years working together on a variety of Intelligence Community activities. Denzil was a solid individual, high up in the organization with abundant authority, and, most importantly, was trustworthy.

Jonathan held his phone to his ear and smiled. "Denzil, good to hear your voice. I hope you and the family are well."

"Jonathan, my friend. It's been too long. And thanks for asking—Ida is wonderful, and the kids are all moved out. We're empty nesters and thinking about moving to the mountains!"

"Wow, time flies. Please give my best to Ida. So, I'm working on a project related to my Blake assassination investigation. I just sent you a plan I drafted via JAWICS. Would love your thoughts, specifically on getting me top cover for this operation. Can you please look at it and then, perhaps, we can meet to discuss?"

"Absolutely—you've got me intrigued. I always enjoy the things you get involved with. Your timing is perfect. I should be able to start looking at it this afternoon and into tonight if necessary. I'll get back to you ASAP."

"That's perfect—many thanks. Talk to you soon." Jonathan ended the call. And he waited.

Chapter 45

Saturday, December 12
The Speaker's Private Residence, A St. NE
Capitol Hill, Washington, DC

While Jennifer set up the early morning secure call, Suzanne was in the kitchen getting coffee.

Jennifer called out, "I've got Jonathan on speaker."

Suzanne, wearing an oversized, comfortable-looking, navy-blue robe with pink, fluffy slippers, walked into the dining room carrying two cups of coffee, one of which she placed on the table in front of Jennifer before saying, "Good morning, Jonathan. What's up?"

"Thanks for setting up the call," said Jonathan. "I just wanted to share with you some details. Have you had time to check your secure email this morning?"

"Yes, I read it at 5 a.m., then called Jennifer to come over, and we both read your plan. You've been busy!"

Jonathan agreed. "Yes, I have. Good news: I've received preliminary approval from the Intelligence Community. All that remains to work out is the final budget and reporting structure. So, essentially, we're good to go."

Suzanne frowned. "I'm not comfortable with the financial aspects. The entire cash thing seems questionable—actually, inappropriate. Let me make this very clear. I do not want, nor will I accept, any monetary compensation, stipends, cash, etc., of any kind. Are we clear on this?"

Before Jonathan had the chance to respond, Jennifer commented, "That goes for me too!"

Jonathan sighed. "I understand that, but just so you know, as mentioned in the report, we do have funds for this. You should not personally incur any expense, and payment for your time should not be seen as a negative."

Suzanne crossed her arms stubbornly. "Jonathan, there will be no compensation accepted. As for expenses, should there be any that we need to have reimbursed, we can discuss that on an as-case basis. Agreed?"

"Yes, of course. We will treat everything regarding funds on a case-by-case basis," agreed Jonathan. "Keep in mind, there are also available funds that can be used to compensate Sylvie as needed. This is typical of any approved clandestine operation."

Suzanne said, "Understood."

"Very good. Okay, ladies, we will be touching base often with updates. I'm not setting a schedule yet. For starters, our communications will be ad hoc."

"Sounds good. By the way, Sylvie is coming for breakfast. We plan to talk to her about her new opportunity," Suzanne told him.

"Oh, good. Please let me know how that goes."

Suzanne grinned. "Will do, double-oh-seven."

"You guys are funny. Talk to ya later."

Suzanne and Jennifer both said goodbye to Jonathan and disconnected the call.

"Sylvie should be here soon," remarked Jennifer. "I'm going to start cooking breakfast."

The house phone rang; it was the Capitol Police security detail letting Suzanne know that Sylvie Bardot was approaching the front door.

Suzanne quickly opened the door. Sylvie stood there in an attractive brown Woodbury jacket, jeans, and her goatskin leather ankle boots.

Suzanne smiled brightly. "Good morning. Don't you look nice! Jennifer is preparing breakfast. How about some coffee?"

Sylvie stepped into the room. "That would be wonderful. Wow, I slept until 8 a.m.! I haven't stayed in bed that late since Thanksgiving morning." She looked down. "And I love your slippers!"

They walked into the dining room, where Jennifer was placing a platter of scrambled eggs on the table.

"Good morning!" greeted Jennifer, her eyes on Sylvie. "Sylvie, take your coat off, and then can you please help me carry in the rest?"

"Of course." Sylvie inhaled. "Ahh, that bacon smells wonderful."

They enjoyed their smorgasbord breakfast of bacon, eggs, croissants, yogurt, and fruit. Then Suzanne suggested they all move to the living room and enjoy the fire.

The three ladies filled their coffee mugs, then each took a comfortable chair and stared at the bright, crackling flames. Suzanne used her iPhone to start her Sonos speakers and selected some classic Christmas music. A light snow began to fall.

Suzanne glanced out the window. "I didn't know snow was in the forecast. How much are we supposed to get?"

Jennifer, always prepared, immediately answered, "Oh, they said just flurries. I love it. Being a Saturday and not having to be in the office—this is nice."

After more small talk, Suzanne decided it was time to focus the conversation.

"Sylvie," she began, "it goes without saying we love the work you have been doing, and let's face it—we absolutely love *you*! You've adapted so well." Suzanne took an uneven breath. "I must admit…" Her voice cracked as she went on, "I feel a closeness to you. It's almost like you're my daughter."

Sylvie's eyes glistened. "Suzanne…that is so moving." She seemed to struggle to form her next words. "I, too, feel incredibly close to you. My mother died when I was five years old." Sylvie paused, trying to gather herself. "I have not shared that with anyone, but it's been difficult for me. Your warmth has made me feel so good—I can't really describe it."

Jennifer, trying to lighten the mood, chimed in, "Uh, ladies, I'm here too."

"Of course, you are! And you, Jennifer, are like a little sister to me," the speaker assured. "Okay, there are some things I would like to discuss regarding the future, which includes a unique opportunity for all of us, but especially Sylvie."

"I'm all ears. I believe that's the American expression, oui?" Sylvie smiled at both women, who smiled back, though Sylvie noted the seriousness behind their eyes. Suzanne's expression hardened as she faced Sylvie. "Sylvie, we have some concerns that perhaps you may be involved with some questionable individuals."

The mood in the room instantly changed.

Sylvie, suddenly on edge, feigned surprise. "Please share with me your concerns."

Suzanne reached for a folder that lay on the floor next to her chair. "Sylvie, here are some photographs. Please look at them closely and tell us if this is you."

Sylvie, staring at Suzanne, slowly took the folder. She opened the folder and looked at the first two photographs, then abruptly handed the folder back to Suzanne. After briefly weighing her options, she realized that she had only one viable choice. Looking at the floor, she said, "Yes, the photos are of me outside of the Russia House Restaurant."

"But you didn't look at all of them," Suzanne remarked.

Sylvie raised her eyes without moving her head. "I didn't need to. I know that the photographs were taken on the three occasions I visited the restaurant, where I met with Roman Mirov, the head of the Russian FSB for Washington." Suzanne and Jennifer exchanged a quick glance as Sylvie continued, "I was recruited by the FSB in my final semester at the Sorbonne. Roman Mirov said they wanted me to be on standby and available for future work. They gave me a small stipend, which helped cover my living expenses, then I didn't hear from them until years later, when he approached me for what he called a fascinating opportunity. And so, here I am."

Jennifer waved her arms. "Whoa! Hold on a minute, you can't just skip to today. Tell us about your assignments, and why are you here."

Sylvie thought fast. "To be honest, I really don't know all the reasons I am here, or what my full purpose is. Last fall, Roman Mirov informed me that my Paris law firm had agreed to allow me to spend an undefined amount of time working in Washington. Mirov later explained that this would allow me to fulfill my obligation to him. My assignment would be to observe and report anything of significance."

Suzanne looked at her expectantly. "And? What have you reported?"

Sylvie shrugged, carefully maintaining eye contact. "Really, not much. I mean, I told him about the trade report I wrote and that I met you in the hospital, that I was enjoying my work, and I always ask him how much longer I need to keep reporting."

Jennifer shifted in her seat. "What was his reaction to your reports? Did he have follow-up actions for you? Tell us what was said."

"He said he was pleased with what I was sharing with him and asked me to focus on being of value to you guys." She looked down, smoothing her jeans as her voice lowered to almost a whisper. "He said he would let me know when I was no longer needed."

Suzanne squinted. "That's it?"

"Pretty much." Sylvie looked up, meeting the speaker's gaze squarely. "You must understand, our three meetings were never longer than a few minutes, and although I never met any others, I believe he was receiving reports from more than just me."

Jennifer leaned back. "From others in Congress?"

Sylvie glanced in her direction. "I can't be sure, but I don't think so."

"How much is he paying you?" asked Suzanne.

Sylvie blinked. "Actually, nothing. I just sort of assumed I was paying him back for the help he gave me while I was in school." She glanced into the fire, her expression filled with shame and sadness.

Jennifer and Suzanne exchanged a look. "When is the next time you'll be meeting with him?" asked Jennifer.

"I have no idea. The way it works is, he'll text me, and then I immediately meet him at the upstairs bar at the Russia House."

Suzanne frowned. "Sylvie, you've given us a lot to think about. We're going to need some time to go over all this."

Sylvie laid her hands on her lap. "Of course." Her eyes wandered from Suzanne to Jennifer, trying to glean as much as she could from both women's expressions. "Oh, earlier, you mentioned something to discuss about my future?"

"Yes, but given what we've just learned, I need to think about it." Suzanne's gaze was unreadable. "Sylvie, I need you to not meet with Roman Mirov anymore."

Sylvie quickly nodded. "Absolutely, of course. I'm fine with that. However, that would make him suspicious, and I'm not sure how he might react."

"Good point," conceded the speaker. "So, for now, continue on, and let's meet here after lunch tomorrow to pick this up where we left off."

Suzanne and Jennifer escorted Sylvie to the door and said goodbye. Once the door was closed, Suzanne said to Jennifer, "We need to get Jonathan on the phone."

. . .

"Jonathan, I have you on speaker." Suzanne glanced at her chief of staff. "Jennifer is here too."

Jonathan's voice came through the phone. The man sounded intensely serious. "Okay, the secure text you sent me was very interesting. Fill me in."

For the next fifteen minutes, Suzanne and Jennifer relayed practically verbatim their last conversation with Sylvie.

Jonathan was silent for a few seconds afterward. "Fascinating and great timing. Did either of you have any doubts regarding Sylvie's sincerity?"

"None at all," answered Suzanne. "Jennifer?"

Jennifer replied, "No doubts. She was most sincere, honest, and forthcoming. I really felt for her. She's been placed in a very stressful situation."

Suzanne continued, "I felt she was completely honest with us. She shared everything, not holding back anything at all."

"Interesting. I had assumed she was a rather low-level operative, but now I believe the term 'operative' may be too harsh to describe her," determined Jonathan. "The Russians are famous for recruiting superior college students, then stringing them along until needed at a later time. Then they have their recruits go through a very gradual and methodical indoctrination. It can take years to develop them into full-fledged agents. All that being said, I feel very strongly that we're getting her at the right time."

Suzanne frowned. "I don't want to place her in any danger."

"Agreed. I recommend we move forward, but at a very slow pace," decided Jonathan. "Go ahead and meet with her tomorrow, and let's start by giving her a minor assignment. Ask her to find out who Roman Mirov reports to. Let's get her working for the good guys!"

"Jonathan, what about the Russia House meetings?" chimed in Jennifer.

"She should continue as if nothing has changed. We don't want Roman Mirov sensing that anything is different. By the way, we've done additional analytics on our surveillance photos. It would appear at this point, Roman Mirov has at least four agents reporting to him here in Washington. We've positively identified all four: Sylvie, plus two that work in the Pentagon, and the last one is up at Fort Meade, in Maryland, where NSA is headquartered."

. . .

Sylvie got back to her apartment and texted Roman: *COMPROMISED, IMPLEMENTED PLAN AS REHEARSED. MEET TONIGHT.*

Chapter 46

Saturday, December 12
Russia House, Washington, DC

It was after 10:00 p.m.; the dinner crowd was starting to thin out. Sylvie and Roman were huddled at the far end of the bar.

Sylvie scowled. "You need to change your meeting location. This place is being monitored. They probably have photos of all your direct reports."

Roman, under the influence of several vodkas, placed his near-empty glass on the bar and motioned to the bartender that he needed a refill. He leaned in close to Sylvie and, in a low voice, said, "Don't worry, there is no way they can track my guys. There's fifteen of 'em! The Americans don't have the resources nor time to track all of them." He welcomed his new glass and took a long drink. After thumping the glass back down, he added, "I will share with you that Command is threatening to make changes to my staff."

Sylvie eyed him. "Roman, that's just politics. You shouldn't let it concern you."

Roman's eyes were down. "I don't know… I've got a bad feeling."

Sylvie, frowning, changed the subject. "By the way, you should not change your pattern of regularly meeting with me here. I don't want to raise any suspicions. They believe I am nothing more than a junior-level worker. Let's not give them any reason to believe that has changed."

Roman, his speech slurred, muttered, "You, junior level?!" He burst out into an obnoxiously loud laugh.

Sylvie drained her one and only drink, then hopped off the barstool, looking across the room. She motioned to a man standing in the dark, far corner. He walked over and stood at attention next to her.

"Corporal, I am placing you in charge of getting Mr. Mirov home safely," Sylvie informed the arrow-straight man.

The man responded with a curt nod. "Yes, Major."

331

Chapter 47

Sunday, December 13
The Speaker's Private Residence, A Street NE
Capitol Hill, Washington, DC

Suzanne, Jennifer, and Sylvie enjoyed their Thai carryout while discussing details on how Sylvie could be of significant value in sharing with them information specific to Roman Mirov. Sylvie seemed more than eager to help while suggesting she really wasn't privy to much detail but would do her best to try to learn more without raising any suspicion.

The three ladies made herbal tea, then sat near the fire in the living room.

"We go into Christmas break later this week," Suzanne mentioned. "Our last full day is Thursday the 17th."

"I know." Jennifer smiled. "I've been counting the minutes. You still planning to go home to West Chester on New Year's Day?"

Suzanne grinned. "Yes! I want to spend Christmas here. I hope the two of you can come for Christmas Eve dinner. Derek will be here too."

"Well, you know I don't have any other place to be," Jennifer remarked, then looked embarrassed. "Oh, wait, I'm sorry, that did not sound nice. Let me try that again." She cleared her throat. "I would love nothing more than to be able to spend Christmas Eve with you, my favorite people."

They all laughed.

"I'm in, but can I take my secret-agent cape off for Christmas?" Sylvie requested with a slight smile.

Suzanne laughed. "Yes, of course. No work, just good wine, good dinner, and great company."

Jennifer glanced at Sylvie. "I don't mean to kill the mood, but Sylvie, you should report to Suzanne what you shared with me earlier this afternoon."

Sylvie nodded and took a big breath. "Yes, of course." She straightened. "In my quest to become a super-spy, I've learned a couple of things. I'm not certain of their value, but I thought you should be aware."

Suzanne waved. "Of course, please go on."

"I had a brief meeting with Roman Mirov last night. It was just a basic meeting for me to review what I'm working on and if I had learned anything that he should report to his superiors. I told him, with the holiday recess coming up, there was a mad rush to get everything done and that people were already leaving town. I also told him I was working on the trade agreement summit that you hoped to host in the spring. He didn't take any notes. He seemed distracted, so I asked what was wrong. He mentioned his frustration over what he calls 'Command.' I believe he means the people he reports to in Moscow. He was angry because they are threatening to make changes to his resources. They don't feel they are getting the value they need."

Suzanne looked pleased. "Good information. Was there anything else?"

Sylvie shook her head. "No, I'm usually in a hurry to get out of that place. It's a swanky bar, with lots of vodka being consumed, so I try to limit my time there to just a few minutes."

"I don't blame you," said Suzanne. "Thanks for the report."

Sylvie's gaze lingered on the speaker. "I'm just curious… What will you do with the information I give you?"

Suzanne didn't have an answer she could share, so she tried to sound nonchalant. "Oh, it'll just get logged. I'm not sure who if anyone will ever read it." She could tell Sylvie wasn't really buying her answer, so she changed the subject. "So, what night is the National Cathedral Joy of Christmas thing?"

Jennifer answered, "Wednesday night."

"I love it. The choirs and bells are always magnificent. Sylvie, why don't you come with us?" requested the speaker. "It really is wonderful."

"Uh, yeah, great!" Sylvie answered. "Thank you."

Jennifer and Suzanne smiled back, looking pleased.

Chapter 48

Tuesday, December 15
Michael's Drive
Bethesda, Maryland

Delun Li and Dr. Zhang finished listening to the latest recordings in the basement room, which had been temporarily converted into a high-tech work room.

"It's pretty obvious that President Gentry is maneuvering everything to us," remarked Delun. "When the Russians figure out they are being replaced, we will need to be prepared for retaliation."

Dr. Zhang replied, "Always good to be prepared for anything, but they won't be in a position to retaliate. With Jonathan Cartwright closing in on them, the Russians' primary focus will be to exit the US as fast as they can. You were brilliant to recommend we not eliminate Cartwright. He's doing more to assure our permanence than anything we could have done on our own!"

Delun nodded. "I just don't want President Gentry to be disappointed that we did not follow through on her assignment to eliminate him."

"Worry not," assured Zhang. "I have conveyed to the president that at this point, we don't need to eliminate Cartwright because our ability to control him for our mutual benefit makes the most sense right now. We will indeed eliminate him when he's of no further use to us. Furthermore, the president is starting to show her faith in us. She has just provided me with some classified details on their nuclear submarine fleet."

"Excellent news. One more thing—I believe we have an outstanding opportunity to eliminate the speaker at tomorrow night's event at the National Cathedral. As a matter of fact, at this very moment on a farm outside of Cambridge, on the eastern shore of Maryland, we're conducting the final tests on our latest drone technology," announced Delun. "I'm really excited about our capabilities. This drone uses facial recognition and can determine its target at a distance of five hundred meters, day or night. The ordnance we're using will have the impact of a grenade, so there will be collateral damage, but I believe we would agree the value of the target is well worth it."

Dr. Zhang smiled. "Indeed."

Chapter 49

Wednesday, December 16
National Cathedral
Washington, DC

The large, black Suburban with its red and blue roof lights flashing sailed up Wisconsin Avenue. The speaker, Jennifer, Derek, and Sylvie were in awe as they looked out the window, watching the large, majestic cathedral grow in size as they got closer.

Derek sighed. "I love it. It really is starting to feel like Christmas."

Suzanne agreed. "It is. I know I sometimes complain about doing this event, but I really do love it."

The Suburban pulled around the south side of the cathedral, and the Capitol Police officer seated in the front passenger seat quickly jumped out and walked around to the other side of the vehicle. After checking with the other law enforcement personnel standing nearby, he opened the side door and helped the speaker exit the vehicle. Then, followed by the others, the four walked to the special side entrance.

Since the speaker was the highest-ranking official attending that night, she and her guests were immediately escorted to their front-row seats. The symphony was playing Mozart Christmas music. As soon as the speaker entered, most in the audience stood and applauded. The speaker, all smiles, vigorously waved, picking out and pointing to various individuals. Once seated, the choir began singing "Carol of the Bells."

For the next two hours, choirs, bell tollers, and the symphony played magnificently. Everyone stood for the final number, "Hallelujah Chorus," from Handel's "Messiah."

While the thunderous applause was going, the speaker and her guests were escorted out of the cathedral. As they walked to their Suburban, a large flash could be seen to the southeast, followed by a loud thud.

They all wondered what it was. It seemed to startle the speaker more than the others. Ever since the golf course assassination attempt, loud noises had really begun to upset her. The Capitol policeman waiting to close their door suggested it was probably just fireworks.

In that same moment, Delun Li could be seen far across Wisconsin Avenue, looking at the sky, frozen in place. Then, he suddenly walked away.

Chapter 50

Saturday, December 19
Manns Choice, Pennsylvania

The image of Denzil Jacobson of the CIA came into clear view on the monitor.

"Okay, Denzil, we see you now," said Jonathan, gazing at the monitor. "I'm here with Sam Poundstone. I believe you two worked together."

Denzil flashed Sam a grin. "Hey, Sam, great to see ya. How's Hollywood?"

Sam smirked. "Ha! You're just jealous."

"Guilty," admitted Denzil with a wink. "I'll promise you this—when I retire in eight months, twenty-six days, and thirteen hours, I'm coming for ya, bud. I want your job!"

"In all seriousness, I would love you out here working with me. It is pretty darn nice. Well, that is, when I get to be there." Sam gave Jonathan a mock glare. "Our friend Jonathan here doesn't seem to allow me to work my real job!"

The men laughed.

Denzil went on, "Okay, guys, I won't take too much of your time but needed to share some updates. The explosion in Meridien Hill Park in DC, last Wednesday night, was actually a grenade that had been piloted by a drone. Fortunately, no one was injured. We've examined what's left of the drone. We believe it's Iranian."

Jonathan scowled. "The damn Russians have been buying a lot of Iranian drones since the war with Ukraine started."

Denzil nodded in grim agreement. "Our analysts believe it's likely Russians, but we don't have conclusive evidence. Our folks are certain that the target was not Meridian Hill Park. Our review suggests that since the president was skiing in Park City, Utah, the only other likely target would have been the Speaker of the House, who was attending an event at the National Cathedral, and the blast coincided with the exact time she was walking to her limo."

Sam digested that. "So, they were only off-target by two miles. Yep, sounds like the Russians!"

"We're working on the wreckage to determine if the navigation failed," Denzil informed the two men.

Jonathan rubbed his jaw. "Damn, they're continuing to try to eliminate the speaker."

"Yes, and considering the mystery behind whatever happened to the AG, we're concerned for you since you've been targeted three times now," Denzil reminded him.

Jonathan smiled wryly. "Yep, I'm getting used to it. By the way, what are your thoughts on Blaylock being AG?"

Denzil answered, "We like him. We doubt that Gentry will give him much freedom to do his job."

Jonathan grimly agreed, "Yeah, she's gonna prevent him from doing much of anything."

"All right, gents…" Denzil's gaze moved from one man to the other. "I'm being called into another urgent crisis du jour. I will keep both of you posted on whatever additional intel we pick up. Good luck, and Jonathan, keep your head down!"

"Denzil, many thanks for everything." Jonathan raised a finger. "Just one thing before you go—we're hearing that the Russian Command isn't totally enamored with the Washington FSB due to their many recent flubs, etc. In any event, Moscow is threatening to make some wholesale changes in personnel, which will impact its presence in DC. Can you keep your ear to the ground on this and see if it might be true?"

"Got it. Will do. I'm off—out." Denzil's face disappeared, and the screen went dark.

Chapter 51

Thursday, December 24
The Speaker's Private Residence, A St. NE
Capitol Hill, Washington, DC

After spending the afternoon emptying three bottles of wine and enjoying the huge meal of raw oysters, baked ham, roasted turkey, too many sides, and great desserts, Suzanne, followed by Derek, Sylvie, and Jennifer, moved into the living room. They admired the beautifully decorated, seven-foot Fraser fir as they sat in the glow of the fire burning in the fireplace.

Derek patted his slim stomach. "Suzanne, that was the absolute best Christmas dinner I've ever had."

"Well, it was a team effort," said Suzanne.

"When did you have time to get this tree," Jennifer asked the speaker, "and who helped you decorate it?"

Suzanne winked at Derek. "I had a little help."

Jennifer smiled. "Well, it's nicer than the one I did for you last year."

Sylvie returned from the bathroom. She remained standing and stretched. "I'm going to call it a night."

Suzanne's face fell. "But it's only ten o'clock! We were going to sing carols." Seeing that she was determined to go, Suzanne stood and gave Sylvie a hug. "I loved having you here with us."

Derek and Jennifer stood and hugged Sylvie as well.

"You know what? I think I'm going to go too," said Derek idly. "I have a mass I would like to attend early tomorrow morning."

They all walked to the door together. Jennifer told Suzanne that she would stay to help with the dishes, and Sylvie and Derek left.

The pair had walked a few blocks together when Sylvie remarked, "I like that I only have to walk six minutes to get to my apartment. Where do you live?"

Derek gazed ahead. "I'm in Dupont Circle. It's a great neighborhood."

Derek's Uber arrived; Sylvie hugged him. Derek felt that the hug was a bit long but not at all uncomfortable. As they separated, Sylvie said, "Thanks for everything. You are a good man, Derek."

Derek nodded, wondering if she was planning on going away soon or something; he didn't question her, instead just replying, "Merry Christmas, Sylvie."

Sylvie smiled, turned, and walked away.

. . .

Jennifer and Suzanne finished with the dishes. Then, Jennifer put her coat on and commented, "I was surprised by the way Sylvie left. It seemed rather abrupt."

Suzanne nodded. "Something's up. As she hugged me, she said in my ear, 'Duty calls.'"

Jennifer frowned. "Oh, boy, poor thing. Well, I'm sure she'll report to us tomorrow."

Suzanne dried her hands with a dish towel, giving Jennifer a long, warm look. "Thanks, dear, for all your help. I love you, kid. Merry Christmas."

They hugged and Jennifer was off.

Suzanne poured herself a snifter of brandy, put on some Christmas music, and sat in a recliner in her living room, gazing into space, alone save for her memories.

Chapter 52

Thursday, December 24
4th Street SE, Capitol Hill, Washington, DC

Sylvie entered her apartment. Per the text she received earlier, Roman Mirov was there seated in her living room waiting for her.

Sylvie closed her apartment door behind her. "This can't be good. What's going on, Roman?"

Mirov gazed at her evenly, his mouth a thin line. "My worst fear—we're being disbanded."

Sylvie accepted this stoically, though her mind was already running through the possible outcomes of this news. "I had a sense this was going to happen," she said quietly. "What are the details?"

"President Gentry is not pleased with our performance. She talked to Putin directly!"

Sylvie's eyebrows shot up. "Oh, no, she didn't! Is he angry?"

Mirov cocked his head. "Strangely, no. In fact, he complimented us, and you by name. He thanked me for the outstanding work, and then he personally listed several of our accomplishments. He said he wants our input on specific plans he has. He wants us back in Moscow. Tomorrow!"

Sylvie couldn't help but be puzzled. That wasn't at all the response she'd been expecting. "Did he say who will be sent to take our place?"

Mirov gazed at her intensely. "That's the problem—no one will be replacing us."

Sylvie was now completely nonplussed. "What?!"

"Command has received intel that President Gentry has recently started working with the Chinese. It was the Chinese that killed the attorney general, and we believe that action on the speaker is imminent."

Sylvie fought to contain her emotions at this unwanted news. "Okay. What's next?"

"Most of my direct reports are being reassigned to other agents. Some are already on their way back to Moscow. I have tickets for you and me to leave late tomorrow. You need to meet me at the embassy at 10 p.m. I have to go now. There are several loose ends that need my attention."

Sylvie put up a hand. "Roman, I need an extra ticket. There will be one more accompanying us."

Chapter 53

Friday, December 25
The Speaker's Private Residence, A St. NE
Capitol Hill, Washington, DC

It was just past midnight; the man was in all black, his face covered with a mask. He climbed over the six-foot stone wall and, with a small flashlight, guided his steps through the rear courtyard. It took him less than thirty seconds to pick the lock on the rear door. Then he maneuvered the two deadbolts open. The man in black stepped into the kitchen and listened. The only sounds were the air from the heating system and faint Christmas music.

He cautiously walked from the kitchen into the hallway and now could clearly see the speaker in the living room. She was asleep in a recliner, an empty brandy glass on the floor next to her.

He drew his Glock 19, checked that the sound moderator was screwed tight, turned on the laser, and released the safety catch. He was less than fifteen feet away. Leaning against the wall, he raised his gun until the laser's red dot was visible on the top of the speaker's head. As he began to slowly squeeze the trigger, two bright flashes lit the room, followed by a scream. The shooter lay on the ground in agony, clutching his hand. His gun was kicked away; then a second kick square to his face left him unconscious.

Sylvie rushed to the aid of the speaker, whose hand was bleeding. She was sitting up and cursing.

Sylvie leaned down and quickly examined her hand. "Thank God you're okay. This is just a flesh wound."

Suzanne looked up at her with wild eyes. "What the hell! Sylvie, what just happened?!"

"Let's just say, I was at the right place at the right time." Sylvie wrapped Suzanne's hand in a cloth napkin. "You should be fine. Looks like he got his shot off just as mine hit his gun."

Suzanne took a few slow breaths, regaining her composure. "What do we do now?"

"You're going to give me a thirty-second head start," Sylvie began, "and then call the Capitol Police. Tell them the entire story—that this guy broke into your house, and just as he was about to shoot you, your staff member shot him."

Sylvie walked over to the man lying on the ground, pulled off his mask, and took his picture.

"Who is he?" Suzanne asked, blinking hard and still gripping her hand.

"I don't know, but he's not Russian." Sylvie knelt next to him, retrieved the hypodermic needle she had in her purse, and injected something into his neck. "There, he'll be asleep for hours. I've got to go."

Sylvie walked over to the speaker. "You'll be fine." Sylvie took a deep breath and looked into Suzanne's eyes. With emotion in her voice, she continued, "Suzanne, you really are like a mother to me. I love you. I have to go."

As Sylvie looked around the room one more time, she added, "Oh, guess what? It's after midnight— Merry Christmas. Now call the police!"

Sylvie walked out the back door, climbed the wall, and headed into the night.

Chapter 54

Friday, December 25
Manns Choice, Pennsylvania

It was just after sunrise; Jonathan and the speaker had been on a secure call for almost ninety minutes.

Jonathan's face on the screen was pensive. "So, that's it? Sylvie is gone?"

"I really wonder where she learned to shoot like that. Bottom line, Jonathan, she saved my life." Suzanne paused. "But the way she left…" Suzanne looked away. "I just know that I will never see her again."

Jonathan sighed. "Well, she won't get far. A nationwide BOLO [Be On the Look Out] for her was posted a few hours ago."

Suzanne, still looking away, shook her head. "They won't find her."

Jonathan glanced toward the far side of his screen. "Hold on. I just received another secure text from Denzil. They still have not been able to identify your shooter. His weaponry was top-notch. He's gotta be working with the Russians or Chinese."

That caught Suzanne's attention. "The only thing I've allowed released to the press is that a burglar was found in my house and is in custody. Nothing about gunshots!"

"Yes, that is best, and this afternoon, I'll be giving them the story of the century."

Suzanne looked uncertain. "You sure releasing the assassination report today makes sense?"

Jonathan nodded. "Yes. As we've discussed, we have no choice. These attempts on our lives have got to stop. Getting the report out there and exposing the president for what she is—a criminal and traitor— should force her to spend all of her time defending herself instead of trying to kill us. And don't worry, Denzil and I did some redactions of the most sensitive classified information in the report. However, we're leaving the most damning pieces about the president unredacted. I should be able to avoid jail time, but that really doesn't matter. To me, at this point, I'll do whatever it takes to get this woman out of office and behind bars."

"I agree." Suzanne took a breath. "So... Wow... Jonathan, we've been on the phone for a long while."

Jonathan looked concerned. "You sure you don't need me to come there?"

"No, I am fine. Jennifer is here with me, and the Capitol Police have small armies at my front and back doors! I have a scratch on my hand. It's embarrassing to consider this as a gunshot wound, and the police are insisting I get checked out by medical. I can have this done quietly at the Capitol Medical Unit. Then, I'll try to get in a nap, although I already know I won't be able to sleep thinking about what happened to me and what will happen later this afternoon as a result of you releasing the assassination report."

"Thank God you're okay."

"Thank God for Sylvie." She paused, then said, "Good luck, Jonathan, and Merry Christmas." The line went dead.

Jonathan's phone rang. He recognized the number from earlier. It was CNN.

He hit the Talk button. "Jonathan Cartwright."

"Hello, Mr. Cartwright. This is Wolf Blitzer at CNN. Do you have a moment?"

"Yes, of course."

"I have my producer on the line. I just wanted to confirm the information you sent me in your pre-release document."

"Before we start, as you did yesterday regarding the pre-release, I need your assurances that CNN will not contact anyone in advance of receiving the full report."

"Yes, and we're prepared to send you an agreement electronically," Blitzer responded.

"Thank you, and I hope you can appreciate my reasoning for doing so. If word was to get out, the White House could prevent me from releasing the report."

"Yes, we understand."

"At three o'clock this afternoon, I will be releasing to you, other select members of the media, and Congress, the complete Department of Justice Report on the Assassination of President John Blake. This report contains specific details as to how President Elizabeth Gentry, with heavy assistance from Russia, orchestrated and oversaw the murder of President John Blake on March 1 of this year. I am the author of the report. I have been working on this assignment for the past ten months at a classified location."

"We have studied the thirty-page summary you sent us, and obviously, we are taking this most seriously," assured Blitzer. "We would like to discuss with you allowing CNN to break this news first."

"Mr. Blitzer, it doesn't work like that. Vetted members of the media will be receiving the report at the same time, 3 p.m. today."

"Understood. One last question. Mr. Cartwright, are you concerned for your safety?"

"To be honest, yes. I am also taking all precautions necessary to ensure the safety of myself and my family."

"Thank you, Mr. Cartwright. We look forward to 3 p.m. Will you be available to appear on CNN later today?"

Jonathan rubbed his forehead. "Let's see where I am later today, and we can decide then. Thank you, Mr. Blitzer. Goodbye."

Jonathan stood up to stretch his legs, and his phone rang again. This time, it was Fox News.

For the next two hours, Jonathan fielded calls from such news media as *The New York Times*, *Washington Post*, *Times of London*, *Reuters, and Al Jazeera.*

At noon, Jonathan and Tina opened the door for Winston, Frank, Brent, Sam, and Greg.

Jonathan greeted them with hugs and handshakes. "Welcome, everyone. I can't tell you what it means to me to have you here on Christmas. Although, I must admit, I never really thought we would be in a government safehouse!"

Everyone laughed.

"Winston, your chef has been working since early yesterday." Jonathan grinned. "The wonderful smells have permeated throughout this four-hundred-plus-acre site! Oh, and Sam, there's enough here for all the men stationed. I only ask that those of us in the house get to go first. I think, later this afternoon, we'll be a bit busy."

Sam gave a thumbs-up.

• • •

Everyone sat at the large table and, for the next two hours, enjoyed an amazing meal.

At 2:45, Jonathan walked into the living room and checked with Tim, his IT specialist. "Tim, how are we doing?"

Tim replied, "In fourteen minutes, official versions of your report will be sent to members of the media, and 535 copies will be sent to each member of the House and Senate. And one will be sent to the White House."

Jonathan nodded and faced the group surrounding him. "Okay, folks, I wish I had some Winston Churchill-like quote, but I don't. I would like to thank everyone that's here, and I hope history judges us favorably, but most importantly, I hope this leads to exposing and ultimately correcting the terrible wrong that has been dealt to this nation."

Everyone applauded.

Tim announced, "Emails sent!"

Jonathan unmuted the TV, which had on CNN, and said, "So now we wait and see."

Frank, Winston, Brent, and Greg monitored their laptops for any news.

Fifteen minutes went by. Nothing happened.

Jonathan asked, "Tim, any email activity?"

"We've received four hundred out-of-office replies, all from Congress. That's it," Tim reported.

"It is Christmas, so thankfully, people aren't paying attention to their email," Frank commented.

The uncomfortable silence continued.

Jonathan's phone rang. He answered. Everyone stared at him. He said into the phone, "I don't care that my car's extended warranty has expired."

The room burst out laughing.

Jonathan smiled. "Suzanne? Hello, Suzanne? I was just joking with the group here." He pouted a little. "Yes, I know it wasn't funny."

Everyone focused and listened to Jonathan's side of the conversation.

Jonathan went on, "So, you've gotten calls, texts, and emails from Congressional leadership. Wow... On both sides of the aisle?" After a twenty-second pause,

Jonathan said, "Yes, I think that's an excellent response. No, nothing on CNN yet. Oh, wait, CNN is displaying breaking news. Okay, talk to you later."

Jonathan turned up the volume while Wolf Blitzer was in mid-sentence.

"…we're just learning that the report is over two hundred pages and indicates with devastating detail that President Elizabeth Gentry was responsible for the assassination of former President Blake. We now have a reaction from the Speaker of the House who is promising an investigation, and we're also hearing from the Senate Judiciary Committee chair that he will formally request a meeting with the Department of Justice to occur tomorrow. There is talk from the Senate leadership that Congress should be brought back from recess…"

Jonathan stepped away from the TV to take a call from an unknown number. After a short conversation, he hung up. He saw Tina in the far corner of the room and motioned for her to follow him, then walked by Sam and asked him to join them.

Once downstairs in the workout room, Jonathan said, "Well, I just got a phone call, and of all the possibilities I considered, this wasn't one of them. The call was from President Gentry. She used her burner phone to tell me, and I quote: 'You bastard, know that you and your family will never be safe.'"

Tina looked worried; Jonathan held her close to him.

Sam was the first to speak. "You will be safe."

Jonathan glanced at him. "Thanks, Sam, but she owns the FBI, Secret Service, and US Military!"

Sam was resolute. "Well, aren't you lucky you have me—because I don't answer to the government."

Jonathan thought about everyone in the house, concerned for all of them. "Let's get back upstairs and rejoin the others."

Sam nodded. "I'll start a plan."

Once back on the main floor, Jonathan, Tina, and Sam watched all the activity on all the computer monitors: people yelling out headlines while the TV was flipped from one news network to the other.

Brent rushed up to Jonathan. "Man! There are already hundreds of protestors in Lafayette Park chanting: 'Jail to the chief!'"

Frank added, "Russia just announced that Gentry is proof that democracy is a failed system!"

"I've got it on good authority that a certain someone is screaming so loud that the White House physician has been placed on standby," mentioned Winston.

On the TV in the background, CNN had assembled their most senior experts in one room. The headline on the screen read, "Breaking News: Presidency in Crisis" as a smaller banner scrolled across the bottom, reporting that "Vice President Johnson has been taken to a secure location."

Jonathan looked down at his iPhone to see a call from an unidentified number. *Here we go again*, he thought, then reluctantly answered.

"Jonathan, this is Wendy. I need to meet with you. The president is losing it over here. I'm worried for the country. And Jonathan, I skimmed the report. I never thought it would get this bad. She has to be stopped. I want to help you."

"Wendy, I'll set up a meeting ASAP. I've got to go." Jonathan disconnected the call and asked Winston and Frank to meet him downstairs.

The three men soon clustered together downstairs; Jonathan filled them in on the calls from the president and Wendy Wolf.

Frank looked surprised. "Wow, this could be the final straw. Wendy knows where all the bodies are buried."

Winston said skeptically, "Jonathan, I don't know. We have to be cautious. I would not put it past Gentry to use Wendy to sabotage what you're doing or set you up somehow."

"Gentlemen, good points." Jonathan weighed his options. "Let me think about this, and we'll talk later."

Chapter 55

Friday, December 25
Saint Elizabeth's Hospital NE, Washington, DC

Sylvie's heart ached, and the closer her Uber got to her destination, the more nervous she became. She had not seen nor communicated with Loretta since escaping the White House during that late-night freak snowstorm last March.

Loretta Fitzgerald had spent twenty-four years working in the White House. Forty-seven years old, never married, she was an attractive woman, thin and of medium height, her now-graying hair usually pulled back into a tight chignon. Never one for makeup, she did, however, have a beautiful complexion. Loretta always wore dark-framed reading glasses that rested perpetually halfway down her nose, making her look like a librarian. Highly intellectual, she had graduated with honors from Vassar.

Fitzgerald was the only person charged (as an accessory only, however) in the assassination of

President John Blake. After a questionable, government-sanctioned psychiatric review, she was found not fit to stand trial, and due to the perceived danger of self-harm, she was committed to the criminally insane ward at Washington, DC's St. Elizabeth's Hospital, where she now resided. Her legal team had twice filed for an early release, but it was denied both times.

St. Elizabeth's was built in the southeast portion of Washington, DC in the 1800s as a hospital for the criminally insane. Over the years, its roster of patients included would-be presidential assassins Richard Lawrence, who attempted to kill Andrew Jackson, and John Hinckley Jr., who shot Ronald Reagan. Charles J. Guiteau had resided in Saint Elizabeth's until his execution for the assassination of James Garfield.

The facility had suffered greatly as a result of the federal and DC governments clashing over providing funding and upkeep. The hospital enrollment recently reached an all-time low. Currently, due to an influx of funding and the fact that the Department of Homeland Security was relocating some of its offices to portions of the old hospital complex, the entire area was under massive construction.

It made absolutely no sense that Loretta Fitzgerald had ended up at Saint Elizabeth's; she was not insane nor was she even remotely a threat to herself or to society. Sadly, she was sentenced to the hospital because no one knew what to do with her.

Sylvie could not fathom what it must have been like to spend nine months in a rundown, end-of-life hospital. She thought back to happier times when the two women had been together, reminiscing over their secret affair that had lasted for close to a year. Though sadly, that time together had often been interrupted as duty often called Sylvie away. Their relationship was so very special; they were deeply in love. Yet, Sylvie was consumed with the shame and the struggles she faced in harboring the tremendous guilt over having used Loretta to accomplish her goal of assassinating President Blake.

Sylvie became panic-stricken, realizing Loretta would not recognize her since her physical transformation from her former self, Annika Antonov. Her hair and eyes were different, and she was twenty-five pounds heavier. The only thing Loretta would recognize would be Annika's voice. Sylvie decided at that point, she would drop the French act, and going forward, she would be Annika Antonov again.

The car pulled up to Saint Elizabeth's east campus parking lot. Annika got out; it was dark, very quiet, not a soul around. But of course, she thought, it was Christmas night; nobody would be here. Several buildings were dark, so she walked to the largest building that had lights on, avoiding construction barriers along the way.

At the front desk, the sign said, "Ring for service." She hit the bell; an older black man sauntered out. Annika announced that she was there to see Loretta Fitzgerald. The old man gave her a clipboard and asked her to provide her information; she filled out her name as A. Antonov.

He gave her a name tag, warning her that visiting hours were over at 8 p.m., but since it was Christmas, no one was around, so she didn't have to leave, nor did she need to wear her name tag. He directed her to the elevator to get to the basement level, room B13.

Annika found the steps and went down one level, walked along a partially lit hallway, then paused just outside of B13. The door was open. She quietly stepped into the doorway of the tiny room; the only illumination came from a small reading lamp next to the bed and a scented Christmas candle burning on the bedside table, which provided a mild cinnamon scent. Annika inhaled sharply as she saw Loretta sitting up in her bed. Her long, unkempt hair was mostly gray. The room was very warm, so Loretta was on top of the covers, wearing a thin, cotton nightgown. Her legs were exposed from her mid-thighs down; she was painfully thin. Annika's heart was breaking at the sight of her. Then Loretta looked up from her book with her beautiful pale blue eyes, her glasses halfway down her nose. Loretta gave a warm smile, and Annika totally melted.

"Hello and merry Christmas," Loretta said with a curious tone. She paused and cocked her head to the side. "Do I know you?"

Annika began to cry; then, in a soft Russian accent barely audible, her voice shaking, she managed, "You used to know me."

Loretta stared intently, then said, "I know your voice. Where do we know each other from?"

Annika leaned against the door. "I always promised I would come back for you."

Loretta said softly, "Oh my God... Annika." She placed her head in her hands and sobbed.

"May I sit?"

Loretta, looking up, motioned with both hands for her to have a seat on the bed.

Annika sat on the edge of the bed and took Loretta's hand.

"I don't recognize you, but it's you, isn't it?" Loretta whispered. "As soon as you walked in, I thought, and I hoped..."

Annika blurted out, "I've thought of you nonstop."

Loretta took both of Annika's hands. "Me too." She repeated more softly, "Me too."

"I had to make these physical changes so that I could get back into America." She then looked Loretta up and down. "You've lost weight."

Loretta smiled crookedly. "Yeah, well, you try eating hospital food for nine months!"

Annika looked down and slowly shook her head. "I am so, so sorry. I owe you my life."

"I've continuously dreamed about what our life would have been like."

Annika said quietly, "I'm here to take you to that life."

Loretta began to cry.

Annika, in an attempt to lighten the mood, gestured to what was in Loretta's hands. "That's a large book. What are you reading?"

Loretta held up her paperback for Annika to see. "*The Solzhenitsyn Reader: New and Essential Writings*. It's all I do in this place. I've read forty-one books in the nine months I've been in here."

Annika nodded. "Do you get many visitors?"

"In the beginning, a few reporters pestered me, but no, no others. And it really isn't too bad here. They pretty much leave me alone. I get three meals a day and all the books I can read."

Annika leaned in closer to Loretta. "I know this is all a shock to you, but would you come with me to Russia, where we can build our life together?"

Loretta looked thoughtful. "Well, let's see. My heart has been shattered ever since we were separated, I've been thinking about you every minute for the past nine months, I'm sentenced to the criminally insane ward at a mental hospital, and now, you want to take me away from all this? Let me think about it." She laughed. "Can we go tonight?!"

Annika fought the urge to kiss her. "That's why I'm here. I have two tickets for a midnight flight to Moscow."

Loretta was numb; she stared straight ahead.

Annika's smile faltered. "Are you okay?"

"This is a dream," she whispered. "I feel like I'm in the scene in the movie *It's a Wonderful Life* when George gets his wish and realizes he's alive."

"Sorry, I'm not familiar with that film," admitted Annika. "Maybe we can watch it together."

Loretta, with tears in her eyes, hugged Annika. She suddenly broke the hold and, keeping Annika at arm's length, Loretta realized in a rush, "Oh, my gosh. I don't have a passport. I don't even have an ID!"

"Not needed. The car that will be driving us is from the Russian embassy and will drop us off on the tarmac next to the plane. What do we need to take from here?"

Loretta looked around the room. "All I have are my jeans, sweatshirt, shoes, and my book."

"Great. Get dressed!"

Chapter 56

Cape Idokopas
Putin Palace Black Sea, Russia

Annika and Loretta held hands, savoring their uninterrupted time together. Gazing on from a pair of recliners on the front porch of the guest house, the two women enjoyed a spectacular view of the sunset. They laughed and clinked their champagne glasses, having agreed to their plans with each other for the next months and years ahead.

The two figures appeared as silhouettes against the large, orange sunset. One was tall and wore a fedora; the other was short and stout. When they got within fifteen feet, the short man spoke, "We have one more assignment for you." It was Roman Mirov. Annika didn't speak, instead just stared at him incredulously. Mirov continued, "You will go back to Washington and eliminate Elizabeth Gentry."

The two men then walked away. Roman looked up at the tall man. "Well, Mr. Cartwright, you know your way home from here?"

Jonathan Cartwright nodded. "Got it. See you soon."

Epilogue:
One month later

In a Washington, DC-based, ultra-secure facility, the speaker's attempted assassin looked through the bars of his solitary cell and realized that was how the rest of his life would be. He longed to be back home in his native northwest China province of Qinghai.

President Elizabeth Gentry

Congress continued to wrangle with all the allegations against the president while failing to agree on the format of the investigation, President Gentry took full advantage of her bully pulpit, making speeches behind the backdrop of the gleaming White House, in full campaign-like mode, traveling across the country making speech after speech in her defense while blaming the media and the Evil Empire—Russia.

With Congress in total disarray, Gentry's approval ratings soared. Meanwhile, the Chinese, enjoying their budding relationship, took full advantage of helping the president with nefarious clandestine operations.

Speaker Suzanne Montgomery

Facing significant challenges from both sides of the aisle, Montgomery gave serious consideration to stepping down, but thanks to a timely, anonymous package she received, which contained intel that gave her the ammunition needed to "corral" her detractors, Montgomery fully regained her stature and once again became a force to be reckoned with. She could never be certain but wondered if the information provided to her was from her favorite former employee who may have been a Russian FSB agent.

Jonathan Cartwright

Retaining the counsel of friend and attorney Frank Osborne, Jonathan was successful in deflecting the many charges related to his releasing classified material. He still was employed by the Department of Justice but was on admin leave. He secretly continued to work with the CIA and even some select foreign entities in his quest to get President Gentry out of office, no matter what.

Bartholomew Winston

Winston continued to enjoy his retirement. His relationship with the former First Lady Beverly Blake recently made the news when they were spotted together at a Philadelphia art exhibit. Winston divided his time between his grandchildren, his working with Frank Osborne in helping Jonathan, and spending time with Beverly in the planning of their wedding.

Roman Mirov

Within one week of returning to Russia, Mirov was demoted and placed into an alcohol rehab program, where he could expect to remain for the foreseeable future.

Sylvie Bardot/Annika Antonov

The individual known as Sylvie Bardot ceased to exist on Christmas Day. She had returned to who she truly was—Annika Antonov. She remained in Russia and was recognized by Vladimir Putin as a true hero of state and was being considered for promotion. She was enjoying some rest and recuperation time at the Putin Palace as she prepared for her return to the US for her latest assignment.

Loretta Fitzgerald

Loretta was living a wonderful life with Annika Antonov. They were enjoying being guests at the Putin Palace on the Black Sea, where Loretta continued her voracious reading and was learning Russian while working on her memoir.

THE END

Acknowledgments

This is my third book and second work of fiction. My efforts could never have been possible without my partner, my wife Isabelle, who provided constant interest, encouragement, and enthusiastic support. I am forever grateful for the inspiration she provides.

There are not enough words to sufficiently recognize the efforts of my sister, Ariane Emery, and her husband, Steve Moorhouse. They spent endless hours reviewing my writing, discussing it, and offering their help on everything from Russian weaponry to various scene constructs, etc. This dynamic duo was beyond fabulous. If there are any successes to be realized from this effort, I owe it to them.

Dr. Alexandra Goldman, MD, and her husband, Dr. Zach Goldman, MD both provided their outstanding subject matter expertise.

I also wish to thank my dear friend and former boss, Stan Kirk, a wonderful man, who not only is one of the best bosses I ever had but also a great friend who took the time to read early drafts and offer encouragement and inspiration for me to complete this project when I most needed it.

Members of my first two books' elite "Sanity-Checkers," the team that provided endless support and helped me multiple times: Christina Beltramini, Brent Brookhart, Chris Fahey, Johann Hauswald, Philippe Hauswald, Edwin Huizinga, Ian Komorowski, Brian Lisle, Scott Paton, and Sogoal Salari. All these wonderful individuals offered friendship, advice, encouragement, and discussion whenever needed.

Andrea Vanryken and David Aretha provided great editing. They were really good to work with.

Thank you to Victor Marcos, my Manila-based graphic designer, for another superb book cover.

Thank you to a phenomenal photographer, Della Watters of WattersWorks & Company for my back cover photo.

Angela Hoy, my publisher at Booklocker; she and her entire team simply put, continue to be beyond stellar!

And finally, I dedicate this book to the individuals who inspire me endlessly: my daughter, Katie, and my grandchildren, Waverly and Parker. This book is for you and the future generations who follow.